# The Side Effects of a Broken Heart

Scarlett Jo-Lai'

**The Side Effects of a Broken Heart**



First Printing

ISBN 978-1-943284-40-5 pbk

ISBN 978-1-943284-41-2 ebk

A2Z Books, LLC Lithonia, GA 30058 www.A2ZBooksPublishing.net

Manufactured in the United States of America A2Z Books Publishing has allowed this work to remain exactly as the author intended, verbatim.

# TABLE OF CONTENTS

# DEDICATION

I'd like to dedicate this novel to anyone who has ever thought about
giving up on their dreams. As long as you are breathing,
it's never too late.

# ACKNOWLEDGMENTS

As always, I'd like to thank God who is at the head of my life for the talent, strength, and courage to step out on faith and pursue my dreams, no matter what. In him, anything and all things are possible.

To my "Charm", I thank you for the drive, determination, and push daily for me to finish this novel. You are so captivating and loving. Any woman will be lucky to have you. Your words have pushed my procrastination out of the window and shown me what true friendship means. Without you, this novel probably wouldn't have been completed. I love you.

To my "Diamonds", There is nothing in this world you can't accomplish. If you are told a thousand "NO's", You find a Yes and keep pushing. Every meeting, phone call, & text message is cherished more than you know. Your big brother believes in every part of you and will help you along the way. I adore the woman you are becoming and awaiting to see what's coming next! We on the way!

To my "Paizbo", I thank you for acknowledging my talent long before the first page was created or even thought about. I remember our luncheon at "Sisters" like it was yesterday. You have always challenged me to remain out of the box and preach to me about how much talent I truly had. It feels good to make you proud. I love you.

To my family, I love you all, unconditionally.

# CHAPTER 1

*Your Pussy is your Bible, Your Money is your Testimony,*
*These Niggas are the Congregation, and You are the Bishop.*
*— Sherry Daniels*

## LOYALTY

As I sat on the red bland carpet in Indian-style watching <u>The Proud Family</u> re-runs, I wondered to myself why I couldn't have a Trudy & Penny relationship with my own mother, Sherry Daniels. I prayed to God and wished on a star daily for the lord to warm my mother's heart, but I just chalked it up as God just didn't get to me yet! In fact, it seemed like the more I prayed, the colder Sherry got. Unfortunately, I couldn't understand why because I made straight A's, came straight home from school, and did everything I was asked to do without a blink of an eye. I did have one question that had been on my mind for some time now and which prompted me to ask Sherry as I watched her approaching from out of the kitchen.

"Here's my chance." *I thought.*

"Mama," I paused, to push up my crooked glasses. "Do you really love me?" I rapidly spoke as if I had a speech impediment as the presence of fear took control of my body from her awaiting response.

I wasn't afraid of her by no means, but her death stare gave me the creeps. It felt like even the thought of me made her give me the ugliest stares and looks. At this point, I had nothing to lose. Either my mama loved me, or she didn't.

Sherry rolled her eyes and stared at me like I had thorns attached to my head. She looked at my shirt and twisted her face in disgust at my chocolate Hershey ice-cream stain on my Tweety bird pajamas. I just couldn't understand why one question ruffled her feathers so much. I was home and comfortable in our two-bedroom Hitch Village project apartment and didn't give a damn about how I looked right about now. Hell, she would go days before feeding me which caused me "To go for what I know" when She wasn't looking or my stomach pains could no longer take a backseat to the reality of my situation. Even with all the snacks that I stole, I was still only a measly 115 lbs. Malnourished was an understatement. The boys at school never paid me any attention because, in their eyes, I was flat-chested, ass-dismissible, and wore red, crooked, bi-focal glasses that was always glossy from dirt.

The only asset that I cherished was my inherited winter-green eyes from Sherry and the ability to hold my head high in the face of adversity. The truth was, I only held my head high to refrain from falling over my two left feet that always seemed to be unpredictable. I was already clumsy and hated to be embarrassed in any way, shape, or form.

"Listen, Loyalty, you're nothing more than a Fuck! And nobody gives a damn about you but me!" Sherry told me with loads of confidence.

I frowned. "What do you mean, Mama?"

It didn't matter how bad she treated me, I still loved her with every inch of my heart. Sherry shook her head at my cluelessness and retrieved her cigarettes from the hidden stash in the drawer.

"For starters, I'm not your mother. I'm Sherry to you, forever and always. Are we understood?" Sherry paused for an answer or gesture.

I nodded sadly.

"Good! What I mean is everything in this cold world comes at a price like you and me," Sherry paused to sit down on her L-shaped Leopard sofa before lighting her Marlboro Red cigarette as she continued, "You were created during my escorting days, so I have no idea who your father is. In fact, the only reason you are here on this earth currently is because I didn't want to spend any of my hard-earned money for an abortion and didn't have a ride to the clinic in Augusta. I tried to drink bleach as an alternative, but your ass is still here. Even though, your twin sister died instead of both of you. So, since I did you a favor by keeping you alive, it's time for me to collect my debt and for you to "pay your way" to live here from now on." She casually responded, drinking a bottle of E&J Apple Cider.

I nervously gulped, not quite understanding what her last remark meant about "paying my way. Sherry's revelation about me having a twin sister that was killed so callously, brought some tears to my eyes that threatened to fall. It also explained why I always felt like half of me was missing. I wiped my misty eyes quickly with the back of my polish-less hands to appear strong because Sherry showed no mercy on the weak. In a matter of seconds, I was stripped away of any normalcy to help me endure this pain in this thing called "Life!"

I had already prepared myself for my dark future and already assumed that I would die old and alone if suicide didn't call my number first, after so many unsuccessful attempts. I was ready to jump head-first into a river but the imagery of Quita, my best friend barely recovering from my funeral was always strong enough to stop me. Quita Smalls was a friend that I kept near and dear to my heart. She was the only person up until this point that loved me with no regards. I hoped that Quita wasn't only my friend because she felt bad for me. I already felt bad enough for myself. Besides, I hated any pity and would walk this entire world alone, if need be.

Sherry stood at approximately 5'7, 140 lbs., soak and wet, straggly long black curly flowing hair, dark chocolate skin, winter-green eyes, thin waist, as her body was only malnourished because she was addicted to crack. In her heyday, Sherry would tell me stories of how she had the sex appeal of America's best video vixen and was loved for her capability to command the attention of any man or woman she desired but struggled with three addictions: sex, cocaine, and money which didn't chronicle in any order.

I just stood there dumbfounded like a deer caught in headlights, trying to take in everything that Sherry was accentuating. I was hoping for the best but preparing for the worst in this situation. Sherry instantly sucked her teeth at my loss of facial expression. Then, she began smiling weirdly as if a light bulb went off in her head, as if she had the plan of a lifetime.

"Do you love your mother?" Sherry asked.

I furrowed my eyebrows in confusion." Didn't you say you weren't my…"

Sherry silenced me. "Never mind what was said, do you love your mother?"

I smiled. "Honestly, more than anything in this world."

Sherry smiled back sinisterly. "Good. A plan of mine awaits you. Now, go clean your pussy, douche if you must, and put on that outfit that is laid across my bed. Hurry up! So, your hair, make up, and lashes can be done in time."

I was glad to be the only child in that moment because I felt it would be pitiful to put anyone else through this foolishness. Something in my gut told me that this just couldn't be good, never hearing Sherry speak so happily. However, I jumped up to my feet and began walking briskly towards the bathroom to shower. I was scared shitless because I didn't know how to prepare for the unknown.

One hour later

"Heifer are you done yet?" Sherry screamed from the outside of my bedroom.

I jumped. "Yes, ma'am I'm coming."

I rushed to the door afraid that I would disappoint Sherry. Feelings of discomfort clouded my mind, body language, and thoughts. I had never worn something so provocative in all the days of my life.

Sherry stood in my doorway smiling awkwardly, as she watched me stand in a black & pink Victoria's Secret lingerie set. Sherry grabbed a bottle from the inside of her tattered bra and began spraying a small dose of her "Pure Seduction" perfume on me. She also applied some pink Johnson-Johnson's baby lotion across my body before she took me into her bedroom to place my braids into a nice neat bun in the middle of my head and to apply some individual lashes. After beating my face for the gawds, Sherry smiled at her creation for the second time in life. She took my glasses off, but I couldn't see, so, I squinted.

"Straighten Up!" Sherry Demanded. I straightened up my posture and attempted to stop squinting.

I glanced at myself in the mirror. Inwardly, I smiled. I hardly recognized the person staring back. I no longer looked like the shy girl that hid from any unwanted attention, but a woman of seduction in my own right that I saw in movies like "The Player's Club."

Sherry grabbed my face and looked me square in the eyes before speaking." There is a John in the guest bedroom. The mission is to go in there and do whatever he asks you to do. If you decide not to go in there and make my money, then, the only thing that can be suggested is that you be looking for another place to stay." She demanded.

I contemplated my options in my head for a few seconds.

"Nooooooooooooooooooooooo……..I'll do it. I don't have any place else to go." I cried.

Well, it sounds like you better make sure you please all levels of his ecstasy and snort a line of this coke to stop your anxiety." Sherry suggested as if my cries only enticed her nonchalant behavior.

I nervously walked to the vanity before picking up the straw and slowly inhaling the line of coke that was pre-cut for me. I had never done any drugs in my life but here I was consuming the very drug that I vowed to never touch after seeing the effects it had on my mother. Instantly, the euphoric effects that ran through my young sixteen-year-old body had me feeling like I was floating and implanting the courage that always came up short.

After swallowing the bubble that was caught in my throat, I continued down the hall in a bliss on a different dimension. My only motivation was my mother's love. I was willing to do anything, even if it meant, the inevitable. I was never presented any family, so Sherry was all that I had to my knowledge.

Sherry grabbed the gold brass doorknob that led to the guest room to the apartment in Savannah, GA, and pushed it open. We both glanced at the old John who laid there naked, licking his lips at the sight before him. I grimaced at the sight alone because he looked like he had worms and no teeth attached to his gums. I swallowed hard as hell and started to put one foot in front of the other, but before I could get one foot in the door, Sherry stopped me by grabbing my shoulder and slammed the door back close.

" Always remember five things even when I'm dead and gone: Your Pussy is your Bible, Your Money is your Testimony, these niggas are the Congregation, and you are the Bishop. You're the predator and they're the prey." Sherry coached lesson after lesson as if she was teaching a class until she felt that I was ready.

"Ma, I don't want to do this. I don't know him and I'm only sixteen." I whined, hoping this would get me out of this nerve-wracking situation, but who the hell was I kidding?

To be honest, I was a virgin and didn't know the first thing about sex. I guess I had better been eager to learn because I didn't have any place to go. I took one of my red tinted mid-back length braids out of the back of my bun to tug on and wrapped it around my finger to calm my insecurities. No child should ever have to endure this catastrophe.

" I don't care what you want to do. Just do as I say. If you love me, like you say you do, then you will go in there and complete this mission or be put out on the street with only the clothes on your back. Now, play with it!" Sherry snapped.

"Yes Ma'am," were the only words I could utter without breaking down and ruining my makeup.

"Oops…I almost forgot, one more thing: Every John you encounter, consider it a role that you play in a movie. Command his attention with your eyes by using your sex appeal to assure him that he is the only guy in the room that you desire." These were Sherry's last words before she got out of my way and allowed me to enter.

Sherry walked away satisfied with her game of manipulation, but she never once considered that it could very well backfire on her. Lord, have mercy on her soul.

3 hours later

My head was pounding, and I felt like my legs were going to give out on me at any given second. Let's not even talk about my hair that was disheveled like I had been in a fight. I know I looked deranged and distraught. What that man did to me felt worse than my monthly. My vagina and anus felt like someone had put them on fire and left me there to burn alive.

At the ripe age of 16, I had never endured such discomfort in my entire life. On the inside, I felt violated, used, and manipulated but on the outside, I was hopeful that now Sherry would shower me with love and praise for being obedient. In my young mind, I felt it was all worth it. If I knew what I know now, I would have realized I was only a pawn in her game of chess and she was playing for keeps. With $700 in tote and $300 for a tip in my bra, I trembled to the ground and passed out from exhaustion and severe pain.

Sherry heard a thump from the hallway and stood up from the sofa to find out where the sound had originated from. Once, she acknowledged that I had passed out from the agony. She shrugged her shoulders, snatched the $700 out of my sweaty palms, returned to her recliner with a satisfied smile on her face, and even did a happy dance. After sitting down, she turned the volume up on her TV and tuned in to her favorite show, Love & Hip-hop: Atlanta. She was a personal fan of Joseline Hernandez because she was an extreme live wire and didn't care what anybody may have thought.

After tonight, things will never be the same. My innocence was gone. This will change my life for years to come. Without love, my heart grew cold daily and I no longer gave a fuck. Lord, have mercy on my soul.

This is the Side Effect of a Broken Heart.

# CHAPTER 2



*Getting my money was by any means necessary. I don't give a fuck about a price. - Sherry*

## SHERRY

The next day…

I know after reading Loyalty's chapter, you have already prejudged me as this cold nasty person. Truth is… I am! I really do not give two shits about you, your mama, or her. So, save your comments, questions, and concerns for Jesus because he is the one who made me how I am anyway. Pray for me! That's all ya'll judgmental asses can do for me anyway or kiss my herpes-infected ass. Yes, I gave birth to her for my own selfish reasons: A come up! Nothing more, nothing less.

I knew with my good genes, Loyalty would come out, nothing short of perfection and boy… I was right. She just didn't know it yet and I never planned on telling her because I was going to use her until she had nothing left. Part of me was jealous of her because she reminded me of my old self before the drugs entered my bloodstream, so many years ago, I wanted to be drop-dead gorgeous again, like her, and not a washed-up prune like I was now. I was never taught how to love and didn't have any love to give her.

My hate for Loyalty ran deep as my soul. She was the total replica of me during my teenage years and every time I picked up my high school year book around the house, I couldn't be more ashamed that I turned to the "Glass Dick" for answers instead of trying to get some help elsewhere. By my looks, you couldn't tell that I was only thirty-four years old because

I looked fifty-four. I too had no motherly guidance or love. Honestly, I wouldn't know love if it were standing right in front of me. The love of my life left me, and I hadn't been the same since.

The moment I woke up and noticed a weird bump on my clitoris this morning, I grabbed my iPhone 6 and set up an emergency doctor's appointment for today for some more medicine to control and prevent another herpes outbreak that I hated so much. God knows, I did. Hell, I didn't even know who gave it to me and wouldn't dare call and ask anyone if they had it? All I know is that it made me stay in the house for a week because I refused to let people mock me or make fun of my blotched or pimple-filled skin.

I jumped up in the middle of itching to wash rather quickly and run out of the house before Loyalty woke up for school. I didn't want her to see me like that at all.

As I sat in the waiting room for Dr. Lewis's office, the memories of my own mother, Beatrice Patrice Daniels before her untimely death crept up on me. God, I hated her ass with a passion!

20 years Ago

The sun blazed on my home girl, Shay and I, as we rolled up a joint on Shay's mother porch. It was a hot summer day in June that I would never forget. Our heads, hair, and hands were wet and sticky from sweat but we didn't care. It was better than being in each other's house with all the restrictions.

Shay has been my tight girl since elementary school. The one I can depend on or rely on any day of the week. But the gag is, Shay was ugly as "Mighty Joe Young" and dark as midnight! To say there was nothing special about her would simply be an understatement. Shay was so ugly that when we went to restaurants, I would show her the newest dishes, so she would keep the menu in front of her face. I couldn't have her taking away my shine if I saw a hot tamale waltzing through. I knew if I kept her around me then, I would always be the best looking out the crew. The good thing about her was she was loyal and solid as they came. Hate me or not, I was going to do me!

I was just sitting there in a bliss, looking at my last report card because I was glad to have graduated with the grades that I maintained through high school. Not for lack of intelligence, but to be cool, "down," and popular. I rarely had beef because they knew I would skin their asses. I couldn't really say that any of those things mattered now because community college will be the only place paying me any attention, well (barely), if I decided to further my education.

Shay and I talked about a host of miscellaneous things until we spotted Roberto, the hood's most notorious king-pin Savannah had ever known. He was so fine, I might add.

Roberto had this "Rico-Suave" thing going on with his muscular arms, low-eyes, tapered sides, and enough waves to make a girl go crazy. I already knew in my heart that one day he would be mine. By choice or force? It was going to be his decision.

"Girl, is that who I think it is?" Shay asked me.

"Uhmmm, Hmmmm." My mouth quivered with thirst.

"Are you going over there to talk to him?" Shay inquired.

"Sure, I don't see, why not?" I answered.

I got up from the step and dusted the back of my outfit off before twisting my hips to the side like I was the hottest thing since Swiss cheese. The sun alone gave my winter-green eyes an exotic appeal. You couldn't tell me nothing with my long black flowing hair, pink Polo off-the-shoulder blouse and a matching skirt that I bought with the money I got from my sugar daddies. The gag is, I never ever gave them any sugar.

Roberto was over there looking like a bag of money. I knew if I was his, he wouldn't have any problem running a check up on me. I carefully watched my prize for a couple of seconds until I began sashaying across the street with the "bow leg" walk to entice him as I approached the passenger side of his 1989 red cutlass Mercedes. My camel toe was in full effect. He spotted me in his rearview mirror and licked his lips at me like I was a snack.

"What's up, Shawty?" He questioned.

"I don't know, you tell me." I shot back, playing hard to get.

He smirked. "Oh, I see. Well, what are you doing around 8?"

"Nothing."

"Bet! I'll be through here around 8:30, so be ready." He confidently spoke, rubbing his hands together.

"Okay," I said with a girlish giggle.

He pulled off shortly after that, doing "80 in a 60" to god knows where. I danced like MC Hammer with Shay in anticipation until we heard Beatrice.

"Sherry bring your fast ass in here before I whip your grown ass. "Beatrice said from down the street but loud enough for me to hear her."

"Okay Ma," I screamed.

I wondered how long she had been watching me because Roberto had been gone for over 30 minutes. I sucked my teeth out of earshot and began picking up my Polo purse to place back across my chest.

"Shay, you want to come over?" I asked her.

"Yea." She replied coolly.

"Well, come on then! I said while grabbing her hand like she wasn't a year older than me.

"You had no business at that boy's car." Beatrice scolded.

Beatrice was a little on the heavy side. She usually wore wigs because she burned most of her good hair off in earlier years. If she paid more attention to her "kitchen" and less on my business, then maybe she can take those helmets that she calls wigs off one day but that wasn't any of my business.

All she did was fuss because she was miserable, ugly, and disfigured. I'm assuming she needed someone to blame between my uncles, Ted, Rossi, Frisco, and me. My uncles didn't get her flack like I did. I heard her rants through one ear and out the other. As long as she kept her hands to herself, she was cool with me because I didn't have any problem tap dancing on that ass. She didn't respect me, and I didn't respect her. I was going to create a plan to get the hell out of here one of these damn days.

Shay and I hosted our own concert in my room in nightgowns along with "Destiny's Child: Live in Atlanta tour DVD without Michelle. I really did have vocals for days, but no one knew that except Shay. In the middle of me performing Beyoncé's "Dangerously in Love" part of the concert, someone turned the knob and intruded during the bridge, pissing me off.

"Well, what do we have here?" Rossi asked as all my uncles paraded together around the bed where we were laying across it.

I was doused with fear while watching them groping their penises through their pants.

"We were just playing around doing a concert," I answered in trembles. "Where is Ma?" I asked.

"She went to see a man about a dog like I am trying to now. Listen to me, and nobody gets hurt." Ted giggled.

We nodded simultaneously, pre-accepting our fate with a seal of death. I silently hoped that Roberto had changed his mind about coming to get me to refrain from witnessing this madness or screams to come.

"Start taking all of your clothes slowly." Ted continued, while the rest of them undressed as well. Our clothes came off as slowly as we could until we were naked as the day we been born. "Turn around and lay faced down." He added.

We complied, holding our breath as we held on to the banister upside down. Our innocence was ferociously ripped away merciless. Shay screamed so loud that Rossi stuck a tube sock into her mouth. I just took it and blacked out. I laid there day-dreaming of being on the Caribbean island with Shay with no worries or cares.

There, we drunk mimosas, smoked ganja, and was waited on by hand and foot, living our best life.

Beatrice opened my door to see the chaos but shut it silently to go unnoticed. I was tied up, not deaf, so I heard the door creep open. I made a vow, right then and there, that none of these motherfuckers were going to make it to see tomorrow and Shay was going to help me. Everyone was getting annihilated, even Beatrice, who was guilty by association. I had never felt so useless in all my life.

After what seemed like hours, they stopped and went their separate ways, leaving us there in excruciating pain. I held Shay close to my heart to stop her excessive heartbeats for the next 30 minutes until she exhaled and was breathing normally again. I ran down my plan to her twice so that she would know what to do when the time was right.

It was 3 o'clock in the morning when Shay and I began prancing out of my room naked into the den where all my uncles were watching "Sanford and Son." We did an 8-count dance in front of them to appear to be sleep-walking and grab their attention which was effortless. Their tongues wagged in satisfaction.

I grinded on top of Ted and licked Rossi's inside leg of his basketball shorts while Shay did her thing with Frisco until I whispered "Time." We grabbed each of their guns swiftly and trained them at each of their foreheads. Their eyes widened like saucers, knowing they had been manipulated and played by the Rookies of the Knight.

"I'm running this shit fest now! Empty all of your pockets and don't make me repeat myself." I commanded fearlessly.

They looked at each other confusingly but did as I told them, hesitantly. Frisco began reaching for something until I put a hot one in the middle of his head, exploding brain matter on all our clothing. They knew by the sight of their brother's head that laid on top of Ted's feet that I meant business. I felt right at home with the gun, unflinchingly.

Ted and Rossi gritted their teeth but knew better than to test me with my trigger-happy hands. Shay screamed. I guess she had never seen a dead body before. I didn't know if she was still acting or not, but I hate to have to put a hot bullet in her ass with all that noise. I shot her the look of death and she instantly shut the fuck up. I was scared Shay would wake Beatrice who I was saving for last.

"You won't get away with this." Ted sneered.

"Oh, but I will!" I snapped back in a matter-of-fact tone.

Shay ran into the kitchen and came back with a broom and mop and told both to turn around before she shoved both of instruments inside of their anuses. I nodded happily and took them out of their misery by shooting them in their napes at point blank range. I grabbed the money off the ground and held it tightly in my right palm.

## Back in my room

"Getting my money was by any means necessary. I don't give a fuck about a price." I told Shay. We clapped our hands together and laughed.

In the middle of counting money, I had forgotten my last loose end that I had to clip. I grabbed the Ted's Beretta off the dresser and traveled to Beatrice's room.

"Wake up bitch," I said, hitting her with the butt of Ted's gun at the side of her head again.

Beatrice jumped out of sleep as if she had a bad dream, but the grim reaper was still present in the flesh. She laughed at me when she saw me pointing a gun at her.

"I knew this day would come. I knew that YOU would be the one to kill me. I saw the way you looked at me like you hated me every day. I'm no fool. But, remember this…. Because I have never loved you a day in your life, you will always suffer from a broken heart.

"Argggggghhhhhhhhhhhhhh!!!" I screamed before shooting her repeatedly, ensuring she was dead.

I continued pistol- whipping the shit out of her. Even though she was already dead. It made me so happy to have her life in my hands and to give her my version of judgment day. I'm sorry but the old bitch had to go.

"Knock, Knock." Someone was bamming on the door.

I shook uncontrollably before I ran downstairs to the peephole to see who it was. It was Roberto. I opened it prematurely because I didn't realize there was blood and brain matter on my clothing. Roberto turned his head to the side and pushed the door opened. Not even bothering to ask me any questions.

"Why did you do this? Do you know you can get locked up for this? What happened?" Roberto rambled off question after question after viewing the two crime scenes, Reminiscent of a horror movie.

I rolled my eyes at his panicked behavior." Those niggas violated me and my friend and had to get their number called early." I answered with no remorse.

Shay stood behind me shaking.

Roberto looked at me weirdly and called someone while rambling my address to the receiver. Within a blink of an eye, their bodies were gone and there was not a trace of blood or murder in sight. Astonishingly, No one ever came looking for them either.

Roberto and I started dating shortly after that. He said, "It was because he loved a girl who wasn't afraid to bust a gun." That lasted only shortly until

I turned the Gun on him when he left me for a younger white girl named, Katauna.

Shay and I still talked daily and hung out frequently. We never spoke of that night again. I was glad those bitches were gone, and I would do it all over again if I had to.

"Ms. Daniels. Ms. Daniels" The receptionist shook me out of my daydream. My eyes plopped open as I snatched my pocket knife out from the side of my pocketbook and flicked it open out of fear til' I realized it was only the lady behind the front desk. I was raised to never be too careful.

"Yes?" I asked, putting the knife down.

The receptionist was speechless, to say the least. She looked like she had never been in a fight or ever had a weapon pulled upon her. She kept her professionalism on and said "The doctor will see you now" before walking away, stunned.

After being quarantined and given my meds at the pharmacy, I felt like the head nigga in charge again and decided to celebrate with crabs and seafood at my girl, Shay's house. I decided at that moment to get Loyalty's "johns" affairs together later.

Shay and I laughed like old times with wine and liquor. We even performed our concert like we used to. I really missed her and realized that we should do this more often. Shay was the only person that I cherished, and I will do so until her last breath.

# CHAPTER 3

*I sell my body just to impress you*
*Even when I sneeze, I don't even get a*
*Bless You! - Loyalty*

## LOYALTY

Monday couldn't get here fast enough for me. It was the only time Sherry didn't trip on me about leaving the house. I couldn't wait to graduate, run away, and never come back. That was a promise. My body still ached from the other night. Sherry hasn't bothered me in a couple days and I was glad. I hope she never uses me like that again.

Quita beeped the horn outside and I started gunning for the door. This house made me feel like I was in prison. She looked so pretty in her white blouse, khaki capris, and some brown sandals. She always brought the hood to her look with those "Quita" bamboo hoop earrings. Her brown natural glow gave the term "melanin" a whole new meaning. Quita was in the front seat cheezing at her phone and rolling a blunt.

The sun shined brightly on Quita and I as we cruised through the city on our way to Groves High School in Quita's 94' drop-top Chrysler convertible while taking turns inhaling a Cotton Candy Kush blunt. The minute Mary J. Bilge's "Be Happy" came on the radio, we screamed and sang at the top of our lungs.

*Oh, I cannot hide the way I feel inside*
*(No I don't know why)*

*I don't know why but every day I wanna cry*
*(Every day I wanna cry)*
*If I give you one more try*
*To their rules, will you abide*
*And if I mean anything to you*
*Would it make everything all right*


*All I really want*
*is to be happy*
*And to find a love that's mine*


*It would be so sweet*


I kept zoning out as the lyrics were resonating too deep within my heart due to Sherry's constant manipulation and bashing that "I would never be anything and no one will ever want a whore like me." Pain was becoming the only thing that I recognized.

Quita smoked the last of the roach blunt and killed the engine before retrieving our things from the backseat. We both checked our mirrors and made a "180" to the bus ramp when Quita noticed her boyfriend, Raquan selling drugs by the buses. I just giggled and prepared to watch the aftermath of this soap opera.

From my view, it was like watching an episode of Tom & Jerry. Quita was 5"11 and Raquan was 4"8. The only difference between them and that show was that they were both guys. All Raquan had to do was whisper something in her ear and Quita would be on him like mash potatoes & gravy.

"Why haven't you called me back, Raquan?" Quita asked with one of her hands resting on her hips and the other pointing fingers in his face.

"Ma, I've been out here gettin' this money. Ya Feel me?" Raquan answered, slapping Quita's hand from his cheek.

"Nah, what I am not feeling is you treating me like shit." She shot back.

Raquan rapidly grabbed her waist and began to plant kisses on Quita's face and neck to diffuse the situation. Quita lost the mean mug and started smiling helplessly. I just shook my head and rolled my eyes.

"You let that nigga slide so much, he thinks he's ice skating." I joked on Quita.

"Ma, you don't even have a man, so, mind ya' business. " Raquan said to me.

"Hell, I'd rather be single than deal with a jiggilo like you. " I shot back with an icy glare through my dirty glasses.

Quita backed away from Raquan and grabbed me by the hand before we were late to class. We came up to an intersection of buildings preparing to go our separate ways to Homeroom.

"Alright girl, I'll catch up with you lata' after school. "I told Quita.

"Lata' girl," Quita responded.

We shook hands and said in unison "Only my true ridas' will understand me, as we put our matching half of a heart tattoo's together, laughed, and walked away from each other.

The bell rang as soon I took my seat in my Homeroom/Literature Arts Teacher, Ms. Hunter. Ms. Hunter walked over to my desk with a scowl plastered on her face.

"What's wrong, young lady, you can't get to class on time?" Ms. Hunter sarcastically questioned.

"I'm barely late. Hunta!" I snapped back.

"This right here is my class, and if I say you're late, then, you're late, got it? I want you in your seat before the bell rings. Do I make myself clear?" Ms. Hunter asked, rhetorically.

I just rolled my eyes before replying "Give me a break. Damn! Hunta!"

"Oh, I got your "break". Since you have such a potty mouth on this Monday morning, you can present your poem first." Ms. Hunter stated before walking away to her grade book.

"Fine!"

I raised myself from my seat, walking towards the front of the classroom. I pushed up my glasses over the bridge of my nose, closed my eyes, and pretended that I was talking directly to my mother. I cleared my throat and began to speak.

*Will you ever love me?*
*I would give you my last kidney, just to keep you*
*Alive*
*With no shame, no dignity, and no pride*


*I would give up everything to be loved by you*
*Even when I thought love came naturally from the*
*Womb*

*I sell my body just to impress you*
*Even when I sneeze, I don't even get a*
*Bless You*

*I never knew love could cause so much*
*Pain*
*I desire sunshine but all I get is*
*Rain*

*Will I ever be worthy of your love?*
*Or will I always come in second place behind your*
*Drugs*

The entire class snapped their fingers in appraisal. Every female in the room could not stop their tears from flowing.

Finally, Ms. Hunter regained her composure to show her gratitude. "Thanks, Loyalty for that very warming message," were the only words she could muster to keep from breaking down again.

I nodded my head at her and returned to my seat quietly. I felt so relieved of letting go all those feelings that were bottled up in me.

The bell rang, signaling the end of the class period. The entire class arose from their seats, gathered their belongings, and began heading towards their next period. Ms. Hunter grabbed my elbow to refrain me from leaving. I jumped at her touch because I wasn't prepared for her to stop me. The scared little girl that I kept hidden instantly appeared without any preparation.

"Yes, Ms. Hunter?" I nervously asked.

"Sit Down, Loyalty, for a second." Ms. Hunter politely asked me.

I instantly started getting a little skeptical about her polite behavior suddenly, but I kept it to myself for now. I sat down at the closest desk preparing for Ms. Hunter's lecture. I felt afraid in a sense because it was as if Ms. Hunter could see deep into my young Soul. Ms. Hunter sat atop her desk before speaking.

"Loyalty, if you ever need to talk or need any help, you can always come to me." Ms. Hunter stated in a serious yet, inviting tone.

"Ms. Hunter, I'm sorry to break it to ya', but not even God can help me." I helplessly retorted back.

"Oh, but He can?" Ms. Hunter countered.

"Oh yeah? Then where is your "God" while I'm lying on my back as grace is leaving my heart?" I curiously asked her.

Ms. Hunter covered her mouth remaining speechless.

I took that as my cue to continue "Exactly, I didn't think so!" I walked away with pain in my heart and the world on my shoulders. Ms. Hunter watched me walk away and said a silent prayer.

"God, you have your work cut out for this one." Ms. Hunter thought to herself while praying for me.

# CHAPTER 4

*I didn't have any fucks in my heart to give.*
*– Sherry*

## SHERRY

I peeked out the blinds to see if Loyalty had brought her fast ass home yet. I caught Quita just in time as she dropped Loyalty off in front of the house. They chanted some type of best-friend handshake and walked away from each other. Quita drove off as Loyalty took her sweet precious time before she reached the front door.

I saw Loyalty look at my car, close her eyes, clasp her hands together, and mimic something with her mouth. She must've been praying that she did not have to perform any services for me today, but the devil is a liar. It was the first of the month and the bills had to be paid somehow. I couldn't work because of a fracture in my right leg so I sat home and collected disability, but it wasn't enough for me. I heard the window creak open and walked outside. Loyalty was tip-toeing to her bedroom window that laid adjacent to the backyard. Before she could even check to see if the window was opened, I gave her a sharp blow to the back of her head and caused her to fall instantly.

"Didn't I tell you to bring your ugly ass straight home as soon as you got out of school?" I angrily questioned her with remnants of cocaine hanging from my nose. Loyalty hated when I get high because she claimed it seemed as if I became meaner. Loyalty picked herself up from the ground. I knew she was stalling to come up with a quick lie.

"Sorry, Ma. Quita and I stopped by McDonald's on our way home. I didn't know it was going to take that long or else I would have caught the bus." Loyalty humbly replied, twiddling her thumbs.

"No excuses! Loyalty, you knew you had work to do for me, I mean us." I rapidly placed my hand over my mouth to quickly recant my statement. I took my hand from my face and continued non-abrasively" Mama just needs your help, that's all."

Loyalty looked defeated and seemed to be in a great deal of pain, but I didn't have any fucks in my heart to give.

"I don't feel well today, Sherry." Loyalty said to me in trembles.

"Non-sense! There are no days off. Besides, I thought you loved me." I said, pretending to cry. I should've gone on to become an actress in my younger days because there was no role I couldn't play.

"Yes, Mama, I mean Sherry, I do, but my stomach is queasy, and I'm on my period." Loyalty replied.

I looked at Loyalty like she struck a goldmine as I thought of the guy in Loyalty's room who paid extra for popping her cherry, but in her case, it would be her period. I snapped out of my daydream grabbed my piton, twirled it, and placed it firmly in the ground while standing in a soldier stance.

"Loyalty Daniels recite our pledge and face me!" Sherry Demanded.

Loyalty straightened up her back, feet, eyes and cleared her throat before beginning to recite the pledge that I created to remind her who to salute.

*The Thot Pledge*
*I pledge allegiance to my legs,*
*To the best pussy in America,*
*And to my Benjamins for which they stand,*
*One Nation, across my ass,*
*Indescribable sex with love, power*
*And Money*
*For all.*

I was overjoyed as Loyalty finished the pledge with defeat expressed across her face.

## Loyalty

I just shook my head at my mother's greed because she knew I didn't feel good. It was all in my eyes. I truly felt weak, but I just smiled and chalked it up as another "L". There was nothing worse that I hated more than selling my body, but I loved to make Sherry happy. Even if it was only temporary.

I weakly dragged myself to the bathroom to bathe, get dressed, and prepare mentally for the inevitable. After experiencing a severe brain overload, I decided to take a bath instead of a shower to relax my nerves. I sat on the toilet as the water ran and rolled up a blunt. Once I became satisfied with the water's depth, I turned the water off and lit the blunt simultaneously.

This bath and weed were putting me in a different place mentally. It was an escape from my unfortunate reality. I closed my eyes and daydreamed of a world with no pain with a large amount of my mother's genuine love for me. In a perfect world, I imagined long walks at the beach, girl time around the park, lifetime movies with peanut butter ice cream, and Sherry just loving me unconditionally. I was so caught up in my fairytale dream that I did not even hear Sherry banging on the door.

"Loyaltyyyyyyy!!!!!!!!!!" Sherry screamed as she knocked on the door repeatedly. I snapped out of my daze after hearing Sherry's screams. I jumped up to retrieve my washcloth to lather it up with soap and quickly washed. I slipped on my negligee and just smiled reminiscing about the dream I just had.

"This is only temporary. Deep down inside, my mother loves me." I told myself while freshening up and preparing to transform into cookie, my favorite vixen who gave me the strength to turn tricks. Cookie made me feel like I was in control. Without her, I could no longer do this.

# Cookie

I mustered all the strength that I had to do what I had to do. I pranced seductively inside my bedroom to the John who looked like one of my classmates from school, but I quickly brushed it off. I turned on my pink "Beats by Dre" pill to Beyoncé's "Speechless" and began to slowly grind to my own rhythm. I was in control for the first time in my life. It was exciting to be the predator that my mother trained me to be. I grabbed the John's chin and looked deeply into his light-brown bedroom eyes before speaking.

"Have you been waiting for me, Big Daddy?" I seductively whispered in his ear, already knowing the answer after noticing the big bulge in his beige slacks.

"Yes!" He timidly answered in a child-like manner.

I smiled at my prey. Vengeance was the name of the game that I played in my head. I knew just what to do to make any man scream like a girl, toes curl, or simply "Bow Down" …

"Strip out of your clothes!" I demanded.

The john rapidly got out of his clothes like he was in a race.

"No! Stop!" I stated.

"Huh?" He asked as in confusion while he stood in one spot like he was frozen as a deer caught in headlights.

"Take them off slowly," I commanded with a black whip in my left hand. He proceeded to ease out of the rest of his clothes. "Now get on the floor and crawl to me like a dog." I continued in a stern manner.

He happily obliged and dropped to the floor. He arched my right leg on to his shoulder while my heel bulged into his skin. His eyes widened at the sight before him. He stared at my goodies and fingered me before eating me like I was the last meal on death row.

I had never seen a man so endowed before which caused me to gasp at his thickness alone. I was sure that he would cause me a lot of pain in the long run.

"Stand up," I demanded.

He quickly stood, anxiously waiting for his next set of instructions. "Pick me up, turn me around, and enter me from behind," I told him.

I knew this was going to hurt, but what's pain when you have a broken heart? I thought to myself.

"With pleasure," he replied coolly.

He did exactly as he was told and held back no mercy!

# Loyalty

"When will I see you again beautiful?" The John asked, licking his lips.

"No need for pleasantries. Now, please leave! You got what you came for." I answered smacking my gums in annoying manner.

The John shrugged his shoulders and got dressed in silence. He threw the money on the dresser and walked out without looking back.

SI got up from the bed & went into the bathroom to wash away the stranger's scent before finding Sherry was sitting at the living room table, snorting a line of coke. I placed the money on the table in front of Sherry.

"Here, Mommy! I meekly said nervously. I always twiddled my thumbs when I didn't know how to ask a specific question.

Sherry looked up from the cocaine she was sniffing when she noticed the scattered Benjamins across the table. "See, I knew you were a gold mine, the minute I had you!" Sherry said, counting each $100 bill silently. I stood there dumbfounded because I didn't know if that was an insult or a compliment.

"Mommy?" I called.

"What? Loyalty, I'm busy." Sherry roared due to the interruption.

"I was wondering… When will I able to stop selling my body?" I mumbled.

"Never, I mean…" Sherry mumbled under her breath and snorted another line.

"What do you mean "Never?" I asked, hearing her answer the first time.

Sherry looked up from the table and faced me with an ice-cold stare. "The day you stop making me money will be the day I stop loving you. Therefore, the real question is, will you ever stop loving me?" Sherry said, using her best version of reverse psychology.

I hurriedly shook my head no to avoid being kicked out and being homeless. I wasn't even shocked at the brutal answer that I received.

"Good! Now, go get ready for your next client! Sherry demanded.

I couldn't move for some reason like what she was saying to me wasn't really registering to my brain.

Sherry got up from the table with her cocaine in a tote and headed to her bedroom, leaving me speechless and in tears.

I couldn't take it anymore. The pain, tears, and prostitution. I couldn't look at a banana without being afraid that it would turn into a trick or John. I went back to my room to write Quita a letter to explain my future actions. I just wanted to remind her that I loved her and would miss her. I decided on the bed that I was going to take my life tomorrow and there wasn't anything on earth to stop me. I hated me. I hated my skin. Just the idea of me made me quiver. Wherever I was going in the afterlife had to be better than this. It just had to. The pressure of my mind caused me to dope up on two Naproxen I stole from Sherry that she used for her leg pain. Rest wouldn't come easy without them. Who was I kidding? Where I was headed, there was going to be plenty of time for me to rest.

Goodbye.

# Part II.

# RAMIREZ SANCHEZ

# CHAPTER 5

*Where is my father when my heart is so full and heavy? You should have never impregnated my mother if you knew you weren't ready.*
*– Ramirez*

## RAMIREZ

I sat on the edge of my king-size bed looking around the room at all my awards. I had earned every basketball honor there was to receive in my city but none of them mattered more than my dad's acceptance.  The only wish I own is for my father, Hector Sanchez, to attend at least one of my games. As star varsity player of the basketball team, there are no boundaries and my perks are endless when it comes to receiving what I desire except achieving that one goal but after 17 years, it was a dream I was ready to hang up forever. Having already taken my basketball team to the championship three times in a row, I had an offer for a full ride scholarship to the University of Southern California, but I didn't know if I was going to take it because I had no family but Hector. Deep down inside, the truth was, I never enjoyed basketball, but only did it for the accolades to belong somewhere, and to appease my distant father. Even though, he never seemed to notice.

My father was also the leader of the basketball team in his high school days, and even earned a contract with the Los Angeles Lakers, but had to turn it down when my mother, Gina Waters, became pregnant. While in labor with me, Gina died due to health complications that caused her to lose a lot of blood. Hector never forgave himself for losing Gina. He had ignored all her calls and text that day because he was messing with a tramp at his homeboy's kickback. Hector had cremated Gina to keep her close to him. Daily, he drowned himself in alcohol and suffered from severe depression. He took Gina's death as a punishment for not being there during my homecoming. Hector strongly resented me because I reminded him too much of his late wife, my mother.

I retrieved all this information through a letter that she left Hector to give to me when I was old enough. I always wondered how did she know she was going to die?

Finally, I gathered up enough energy to get up off the bed to try and get my school clothes out for tomorrow. It was already too much lingering on my mind as it is. After taking care of my hygiene and getting dressed for bed, I jogged downstairs to the kitchen where my dad was coming from the back door with a case of beer in tote.

I was already dreading senior year because this was the year that parents played a significant role in their child's life. But technically, I had none.

"It sucks to be seventeen right now!" I thought.

"What's up, Dad?" I happily greeted my father as I began pouring a bowl of frosted flakes cereal before I traveled to school.

"Hey," Hector dryly replied.

Hector was dressed in a simple, worn-out black Fil-A jogging suit, with his silky straggly hair swooped in a ponytail that had seen better days. Hector sat on the stool closest to me and sighed as if the three flights of stairs he ascended up on had taken a toll on his over-weighted body. I stood diagonally from him, debating whether to invite Hector to one of my games again when I already knew the answer, but I decided to ask anyway. Hector noticed I was in deep thought and decided to beat me to the punch.

"Yes, Mijo?" Hector asked irritably in his deep Spanish accent.

"Hmmm, I was wondering, would you like to come to my championship game on Thursday?" I asked, breaking out in a sweat.

"No can-do Chico, the walking dead comes on Thursdays' and the finale is this Thursday which is why I can't miss it." Hector nonchalantly answered.

I walked away defeated. My feelings were a mixture of anger, sadness, and depression. I missed my mother terribly but hated her at the same time for leaving me alone to live with this cruel sperm donor. While on the heel of my feet, I turned back around, heading back for this shadow of a man. Tears spewed from my eyes with every step as I angrily approached his target.

"Why do you hate me so much?" I roared with so much anger and anxiety.

Hector just sat there silently. He was unwilling to move because he was too afraid to suffer the consequences of making any sudden movements. Hector was stunned at the emotional state of mind that I was displaying. He chose his words very carefully before responding.

"I don't hate you, Mijo." Hector falsely stated with volumes of untruths.

"Yes, you do! You have never told me you loved me. You have never been to any of my games. You barely even make sure I eat, and you always look at me with so much resentment." I revealed, after years of pent-up frustration.

Hector grew extremely angry, jumped up from the sofa, ran to the wall and boxed a hole inside of it before falling with his face in the palm of his hands.

"I don't hate you. I resent you because, in a way, you killed Gina, and if we aborted you, she would still be here." Hector replied.

"I did not kill my mother. How can you place that blame on me?" I asked, clenching my fist, and beating my chest as if I was ready to attack like a pit-bull whose meal is being disturbed.

"I HATE YOU!" I screamed.

"I hate you, too!" Hector said, returning my glare. My phone rang, interrupting our face-off. We both walked away with heavy hearts wondering, "Why does love hurt so much?"

The thoughts that danced in my mind caused me to toss and turn all night. I woke up at dawn due to the unbelief that clouded my heart.

"How could my father blame me for the death of my mother?" I thought to myself.

I groggily got up, handled my hygiene before deciding on some black H&M jeans, a Tupac sweatshirt, and some black high-top vans. Once I was satisfied with my look for today, I headed towards the kitchen because my stomach was grumbling. I opened the refrigerator to find a half gallon of whole milk, so I decided on a bowl of oatmeal. I never noticed that Hector crept up at the kitchen table and was reading a newspaper while eating an apple, which caused me to jump when he spoke.

"Good morning, Ramirez." Hector calmly greeted.

"Sup?" I nonchalantly replied.

Hector swallowed and responded. "Son, I really didn't mean what I said last night, and I do l.ov....... e you." Hector stammered to get out.

"Save it! Hector! You can't even look me in my eyes when you talk or tell me without stuttering." I said with disgust in my eyes and tone.

I threw the bowl of oatmeal against the wall and ran out of the house.

Dark gray clouds and heavy rain dressed the sky as I cruised to school in my 1993 Red Cutlass Chevy Camaro that my mother left me after her sudden death. I drove dazed out of my mind until I noticed a girl standing on the edge of the roof of the school's gym while turning into the school's parking lot. She looked like she was about to commit suicide.

Thinking quickly on my feet, I jumped out of my car and ran rapidly to the back of the emergency stairway that led to the roof. I tried to be as quiet as possible not to alarm her. Reaching the roof's door, I eased it open to remain in the young girl's blindside to stop her from leaping. Everyone looked on in shock at the girl an inch from falling and I silently wondered "What could be that bad that would make her commit suicide?" I noticed all the students, teachers, and superiors stand in silence. It was her deranged deposition that caused me to rapidly jump into action.

"Awwwwwwwwwwwwwwwwwwwwwwwwwwww!" The crowd screamed after seeing the young girl slip off the edge of the roof, almost falling to her demise, but managed to grab on to the very end of the school's flagpole that hung on the side of the building. She instantly snapped back into reality.

"Help Me!!!!" She panicked. The entire student body gasped at the sight before them while the young lady helplessly dangled from the pole.

"Give me your hand, Miss, I will help you." I calmly persuaded her. She struggled to reach for my hand. I had never seen this young gem ever in my life.

"Gotcha!" I stated while pulling her up with a tight firm grip until she made it over the rooftop.

The struggle to breathe was becoming a task all on its own for the both of us. Everyone clapped in applause that someone saved the troubled young girl's life. After regaining my composure, I turned to face the most naturally beautiful girl I had ever seen.

"What is your name? Beautiful?" I asked.

She took her glasses off, cleaned them and stared back at me like she was still trying to collect her thoughts after that nightmare.

"Uhhhhh….my name is Loyalty Daniels. What is yours?" She stuttered.

"Ramirez, Ramirez Sanchez What is a pretty girl like you doing, trying to kill yourself?" I seriously inquired.

Her smile rapidly turned to a scowl as she answered "If I gave you my shoes to walk in for one day, you would return them free of charge so do not judge me! No one knows the pain I have been through to get to this point." She shot back with intensity.

Quita, one of the most popular girls at school burst through the door gunning for I guess, Loyalty. Loyalty interrupted her tongue lashing that she was giving me and faced Quita.

"Sis, are you okay? Why would you try to leave me when you know you are all that I have? Please, do not ever scare me like that again. I love you so much." She said in one breath in the middle of tears.

"I love you too, Qui! I promise I won't do that again. I don't know what got into me. If it wasn't for Mr. Ramirez here, I was sure to be a goner by now." Loyalty said, pointing at me.

Quita must've forgotten I was standing behind them as she turned around with a lost look on her face. "Thanks for saving my girl, Superstar!" Quita praised me happily.

Quita was a cheerleader for the basketball team. I met her during her first year of high school and was silently my #1 fan. She was known for wearing the most exotic hairstyles and colors.

"No problem, Ma. You are welcome. Loyalty, do me a favor and stay off rooftops." I joked.

Loyalty put her head down and smiled shyly.

"Qui, why haven't I seen this diamond in the rough around here before?" I asked curiously.

"Maybe because you don't come to class. Now, that I'm able to put a name to a face, I always hear your name called in Ms. Hunter's class but you're always absent." Loyalty joked back.

"Respect!" I responded with my hands up like "Don't fight me."

"Right." They said together.

"Well, Ms. Loyalty, are you okay to go to class?" I asked with concern.

"Yes, I'm fine. Thanks again." She answered.

Loyalty gave me a kiss on the cheek and walked away holding Quita's hand. I held my cheek where the kiss landed and blushed.

"Oh, Ms. Loyalty, our conversation isn't over either," I yelled behind her. She turned around, smiled, and nodded before proceeding to the door.

I wanted her bad and was going to do whatever it took to get her.

"Nice of you to join us since you only seemed to visit one day out of the whole semester." Ms. Hunter sarcastically said to me.

I smirked, boyishly "Hello' to you too, Ms. Hunter. Now, you know you are the yin to my yang. I can't go this whole school year without seeing your beautiful face." I replied bashfully. She walked away trying not to smile but was failing miserably.

I looked around the classroom for an empty seat until I decided on one that suited my best interest. Loyalty gasped when she noticed I was heading her way to the empty seat beside her. She must've just gotten into a good climax of the novel that she was reading because she looked spook as if she had seen a ghost.

"I told you we had unfinished business, Ms. Daniels. What are you reading, if you don't mind me asking?" I asked.

The novel was getting wet because her palms were becoming extra sweaty. I think I scare her for some reason, but this was flattering to me.

"Lol! I know. I just didn't think it would be so soon and it's titled: The Scars of a Faggot by Kadeem Chabrielle. He's one of my favorite authors." Loyalty said with a smile. I just began to stare into Loyalty's eyes until Ms. Hunter stopped me with her hands on her hips.

"Even though I'm flattered to be your yang, the class is waiting for your presentation to begin." She smartly shot back. Everyone laughed in unison.

"Well, without further ado," I answered without an ounce of fear.

"I'll be right back," I whispered to Loyalty, causing her dimples to appear.

After reaching the front of the classroom, I exhaled and closed my eyes. I was ready to reveal my truth of resentment, the grief of my mother, and my enticing desire to be loved.

*Who Do You Think That You Are?*
*How could you blame me for the death of my mother?*
*You worthless coward!*

*Is it because you are mad that my mother was dying, and you were whoring*
*while she was in labor, portraying to be Mack Man of the hour?*

*How could you look me in the eye?*
*With no pride by your side*
*And tell me you wish I wasn't alive.*
*Like why?*

*How can I love who I am?*
*When my flesh and blood curses my entire existence.*
*There's nothing worse than living under your roof as if I'm serv-*
*ing a lifetime death sentence.*
*Where is the one I should call "my father" when my heart is so full*
*and heavy?*
*You should have never impregnated my mother if you knew you*
*weren't ready.*

I ended the poem with tears flowing freely from my pupils. There was nothing I desired more in this world than to be loved. I swiftly walked out of the classroom and left the standing ovation I was getting behind to regain my composure. Loyalty ran out of the classroom behind me. She found me crouched over and tugged my elbow.

"Hey, are you okay?" She genuinely asked.

"Yes, I'm cool. Don't think a nigga soft because I got a little dust caught in my eyes. I famously smirked.

Then it happened: our eyes connected as if we were floating on a sea in bliss like a total eclipse of the hearts. It seemed like the love we lacked in our personal lives, we could find in each other. I grabbed her chin and pulled her in for a long, warm kiss. Our tongues locked devilishly. I wanted this moment to last forever.

Ding! Ding! Ding! The bell rang, breaking our embrace, but we remained in a tight hug.

"Hmmm… Uhh….Well, I got to get to my next class!" Loyalty stuttered, struggling to pull away from me.

"I know. Me too. When will I see you again?" I asked.

"Whenever you like, Mr. Sanchez." She stated.

"Well, my homeboy Freddy B's is having a kickback in the landings on Saturday. You and Quita should come through.

"Hey, you never know, we may 'pull up'." She flirtatiously stated before strutting to her next class.

## Loyalty

"What got you "cheezing" so hard?" Quita asked while side-eyeing me. She knew me so well.

"Girl, I don't know what it is, but it's something about that Ramirez character, who saved my life by the way." I cheerfully blushed. "Guess what else?" I continued.

"What?" Quita asked, covering her mouth for the tea.

"We got invited to Freddy B's party on Saturday night." I teased. Quita eyes widened as we both screamed together.

"Well, Alrighty then. Let's hop in this whip, cruise to the mall, and find us something sexy to put on." Quita suggested.

"I'm always ready to shop til' we drop and may the fattest pocket win." I shot back. We slipped on their matching pink Ray-bans and drove to the mall.

Quita already knew that I didn't have any money, but she never made me feel like a charity case. She made me feel like everyone else. When I was with her, I was around the way girl just kickin' it.

I don't know what I would do without my girl, Quita. She took me to the mall to get me whatever I wanted within her budget. She even bought me some contacts to bring my eyes out of those dirt-filled glasses that always seemed to be glossy. I picked out some clear ones because my eyes were already poppin'.

When we finally arrived at the house, my arms grew tired from carrying all those bags to the front door where Sherry awaited me.

"Ugly, where in the hell do you think you are going with those bags?" Sherry angrily questioned me.

"Quita and I are going to Freddy B's party tomorrow," I said, twirling my braids and pleading with my eyes that I didn't have to tell Quita that my plans were canceled.

"No, you are not. You have six clients tomorrow." Sherry stated, pointing her finger at me.

"Ma, Loyalty got to live too. I will not be your whore forever." I said, barely above a whisper.

Sherry paused like she was shocked. It looked like she was attempting to make her eyes water.

"What? Better yet, who have you been talking to that have caused you to talk to me like that?" Sherry asked.

"Nobody, Ma." I lied with thoughts of Ramirez invading my mind causing me to smile before moving forward. "I do love you, but, when will my debt of your love be paid in full?" I seriously inquired.

"Well, then, I guess I'll stop loving you, you little bitch." Sherry folder her arms. She was grinning at my confused expression.

"Okay, Ma. I'll do it." I whined.

"I'm glad you have changed your mind. You are off today, so, use your time wisely. She stated with satisfaction.

"Gee, thanks." I sarcastically mocked in the middle of walking away to my bedroom.

I threw my bags across the bed as tears cascaded down my face. I turned over and powered off my 5:00 p.m. alarm setting on my clock that signaled Oprah was coming on. I aimlessly looked at the TV until I heard Oprah discussing important things that caught my ear.

"You have to take control of your life. Stop selling your soul for love. Before you begin to give your love away, you need to ask yourself "Is love being returned to you?" Don't you ever allow anyone to make you feel bad about anything you have done in your past, who you are, or who you are not? People will have you thinking that hate is the 2019 form of love, but I'm here to tell you, it is not. Your soul is rooting for you." The words of Oprah resounded in my heart.

I was becoming strongly encouraged to "Never Give Up". The segment continued and eventually put me to sleep. "A change has got to come" was my last thought.

# CHAPTER 6



*"Fuck these niggas til' it's time to fuck these niggas." - Quita*

## LOYALTY

Saturday Night

"Can we kinky tonight?" SWV's 1997 hit song from the Booty Call soundtrack blasted through the pioneer speakers as the crowd flaunted their sexiest moves they could muster on their partners. Quita and I danced the night away together like we had no cares in the world. Even though that was the farthest from the truth.

My rich caramel skin glistened under the fluorescent lights as I shook what my mama or whatever she wanted to be called gave me. I was clad in a beautiful floral dress, BCBG 6-inch nude stilettos, and a tight knotted bun that accentuated my high cheekbones. Quita was also "shining bright like a diamond" clothed in a coral sequenced floor length dress, Gucci sandals, and a silk pressed wrap that stuck to her body due to the workout she was doing on the dancefloor.

"Girl, I'm so glad that you came out tonight with a sistah. I would have been holding a corner of one of these walls if you didn't." Quita said, smiling at me.

Her statement reminded me that I snuck out when Sherry went to Shay's. Quita was having a hard time removing her hair that got stuck in her diamond encrusted hoop earrings.

"It is no problem coming to hang out with my girl. It was a hassle, but there is nothing in this world I wouldn't do for you. We are girls forever." I replied as I silently reflected on Sherry's bullshit for today. We continued to dance with sweat escaping from our pores. "Overheated" was an understatement.

"Are ya'll ladies having a nice time tonight?" Raquan asked, wrapping his arms around Quita's waist causing her to blush uncontrollably. My face clenched in disgust. I was starting to think that maybe my girl was brainwashed or retarded to eat this nigga's shit every day.

"Man, Quita, please don't tell me you back with this square ass nigga, especially how this nigga carried you the other day," I asked, confused.

Quita just simply smiled, silently confirming what I already knew.

" I don't even understand the half of ya'll relationship. Every time I turn around, he's entertaining these other bitches. You might be smiling today, but when you're crying, I'm the one wiping away your tears tomorrow. I nagged.

"Lo, I'm back with him, but you already know our motto: Fuck these niggas til' it's time to fuck these niggas." We laughed together and shook hands. Raquan side-eyed Quita.

Our favorite song came on, Beyoncé's sexy slow jam "Dance for You". We both screamed and ran back to the middle of the floor leaving Raquan in the dust. The rhythm of our bodies complimented each other to the point we looked like lesbians in a wave-like motion.

I came to a halt mid-song when someone with peppermint scented breath began whispering in my ear.

"We really got to stop meeting like this." This stranger cooed seductively in my ear canal as he grabbed a hold of my waist.

My hands began to sweat profusely once my brain registered whom the voice belonged to. He slowly pulled my body into him from behind and instructed me to grind into his crotch.

Quita watched on with her hand covering her mouth in awe at Ramirez and I seductive interaction. As King B's song quietly faded out, I turned around to find the prettiest gray eyes staring back at me.

"What are you doing here?" I asked with my eyebrows furrowed.

"In hope that I would've seen you again." He grinned.

I was in a bliss of this moment. It was in our eyes that we desired each other. I couldn't decide whether it was the mint scent that lingered from his breath or the men's pure seduction fragrance he was wearing or both were warming my nose and panties. I wanted him bad and NOW!

Ramirez was casually dressed in an orange plaid buttoned-up polo shirt, black true religion jeans that hung slightly below his waist and some black Tim's to complete his ensemble. His beautiful hair was laid in waves. He matched my fly perfectly. I got so wrapped up in this love trance that I forgot all about Quita.

"Hey, where's Quita?" I asked, looking around the room.

"She stepped off to get us some drinks." Ramirez mischievously smirked. I couldn't help but get lost in his gray eyes again.

"Hey girl, I got you a drink," Quita said, coming out of nowhere while handing us our drinks simultaneously.

"Thanks chick," I said.

"Appreciate it, Fam." Ramirez chimed in.

"Fasho." Quita nodded to both of us.

Quita busied herself by scanning the crowd until something drastic caught her attention because she developed this weird expression on her face, so I followed her eyes to see what had her in a still-like motion.

"Lo, please don't tell me that is who I think that is," Quita stated hesitantly.

I broke my embrace and finally saw what had Quita's attention which caused me to spit out my drink.

"What the hell are you doing here, when you have work to do at home?" Sherry yelled over the music in front of us.

I was on the verge of vomiting in disgust of Sherry's choice of clothing. Sherry was dressed like nobody loved her in a "Barbie-Doll" designed nightgown, pink "Bionic-Bunny" slippers, and red rollers adorning her whole head with a pink wrap that graced the circumference of her scalp. Not to mention a Jazz Black & Mild dangling from her mouth.

"I told you that I was going out," I replied.

The only thing I could do was pray to God for Sherry to go home. Words couldn't express how embarrassed I was with my mom coming down here like this. Ramirez still hung behind me like a bodyguard which I thought was the sweetest thing ever.

"Bitch, I told you, "NO!" so you better come on before I disrespect you in front of your little friends, Loyalty! I have clients lined up for you at home." Sherry demanded with her hands resting on her hips.

I thought back on the words from Oprah, narrowed my eyes and clenched my hands in a tight fist. On this day, I decided enough was enough.

"I'm not going anywhere," I said with finality, crossing my arms against my chest.

Then, all hell broke loose. Sherry grabbed me and put me in a headlock before throwing me to the ground. I swept my leg behind hers and caused her to lose balance. I hopped up on top of Sherry and began to pounce on her relentlessly until Ramirez grabbed me from behind and dragged me to the back room with mascara running down my face. The music stopped abruptly with all eyes focusing on the mayhem. I hit her so hard I scared myself.

Sherry lifted herself from the ground defeated before attempting to fix herself up. "You're going to wish you hadn't done that," Sherry screamed at me with anger dancing in her eyes.

"Awhhhh, shut the fuck up! I would've tapped that ass too." Quita replied before shoving Sherry's shoulder and pushed her back to the ground. Satisfied with her work, Quita playfully sashayed and walked away to check on me.

"You okay, sis?" Quita asked, looking at my face. No matter what, that girl always had my back and I will always have hers.

Ramirez was patting my lips with a gauze from a first aid kit to stop it from bleeding. Looking into his eyes, I almost forgot we were in some private room. He was so thoughtful and didn't even flinch at this new vision of me. I tried to put my bun back together, but my braids already fell out of it, so I just let them hang. I felt bad because I didn't want to introduce this side of my life to him. Sherry really showed her ass, and this was no way to handle this situation.

"Yes, I'm fine," I replied, smiling.

"Good, cause if you weren't I was about to go back in there and fuck some shit up. TF?" She shot back, clapping her hands repeatedly.

After knowing her for years, I knew she meant serious business.

"Stand down, pit bull. Not this time." We laughed.

"Y'all both too pretty to be fighting. However, the way that you both take care of each other, there was no room for a rematch." Ramirez said.

"When you live the life we live, you must always be trained to go," Quita responded.

We left the party and went to the Waffle House. There, we shared some embarrassing stories, life-long lessons, and funny moments. This was the first time ever I truly felt like I had a family and I hope this feeling never ended.

# CHAPTER 7



## LOYALTY

"Damn!" I said, wincing in pain.

I sat on the toilet seat and patted my lips with gauze until I noticed all the blood leaking on the napkin from the open wound on my mouth. I couldn't explain the embarrassment, and anger that plagued my heart. I was almost to my wit's end with this bullshit. It was only so much that my young heart could take.

My reflection in the mirror alone scared the shit out of me. My bun was ruined, and my left eye was closed shut, but I knew Sherry looked much worse wherever the hell she was. I hadn't seen her since last night.

Visions of Ramirez plagued my mind and caused me to get a little sad when I played the memories of last night in my head leading up to the showdown with Sherry. I had made up my mind to never talk to Ramirez again and gave up the idea of us ever being together. I weakly got up off the bed to take care of my hygiene as my head hung low.

After leaving the restroom, I walked slowly to the kitchen to take care of my growling stomach before deciding on a box of chicken fries and potato wedges. I poured the grease into the frying pan and jumped when I heard the boisterous laughter that erupted from Sherry's room. I silently tip-toed across the house to Sherry's room, noticing the door was already cracked which made it easy for me to eavesdrop.

"I hate that little bitch with a motherfucking passion. You hear me? She's an ole ugly dumb ass bitch. This hoe thinks because her little naïve ass sells her body to increase my income that I will start loving her whoring ass. I'm her pimp, she's my hoe, if she stops selling that ass, she got to go." Sherry singed playfully into the phone.

Tears erupted from my eyes like a volcano. My heart was truly broken as the one thing I desired was already being taken away from me. I was fed up with everything and everyone. I raised my right leg and kicked the door open, scaring the shit out of Sherry.

Sherry accidentally hung the phone up out of fear. She looked as if she had seen a ghost. I stood in a defense stance, stone-faced with my hands balled up in fists, resting by my side. I didn't know my next move, but I knew this shit was ending today. Someway, Somehow. It no longer felt like the both of us could still exist in the same house. Betrayed wasn't even the word to express how I felt. I think Sherry was ready for round two of me tapping that ass and I was going to give it to her.

"Bitch! You tricked me. You allowed a total stranger to take advantage of me and take my virginity over some get rich money scheme that you created. All I ever asked you for was your love, but now I see, you had no love to give. I said, spit spewing with every word.

The silent treatment Sherry was presenting was enraging me because I charged at her and started throwing vicious blows to her face and torso. "I fucking hate you! You are conniving, deceitful, and sorry waste of ovaries." I continued to insult her between my combos.

"I'm sorry! Loyalty, please stop!" Sherry managed to say with the last bit of oxygen that she was inhaling between breaths, but her pleas were only making me hit even harder, falling on deaf ears.

"No, you are not fucking sorry. Were you sorry when you heard me scream-ing from the other room while my hymen was being broken? Were you sorry for collecting all that money? Ohhhhhh, let me guess, now......you want sympathy?" I laughed hysterically. "Bitch Bye! You let those men do whatever they wanted to do to me over a C-note. I'm your daughter, your fucking daughter." I screamed at the top of my lungs.

I jacked Sherry up by the collar before dropping her to the carpet. I ran to the kitchen and returned with a butcher's knife. I was trying to kill her. If Sherry knew what's best for her then, she had better be playing hide and seek. The aroma of burning grease or the smoke detector didn't even deter me from returning so fast. When I returned to her room, Sherry wasn't in the same spot that I had left her, but I still heard the excess breathing and wheezing coming from somewhere in the room.

"Come on, Bitch!" I said while wheezing myself.

## Sherry

I took my revolver off safety and aimed it towards her direction as I hid in my closet. I knew that she heard the gun cocking back when she said, "If you shoot, aim to kill because if you don't, I will." Loyalty said, unfazed.

"Don't make any sudden movements or I'm going to shoot," I uttered, fidgeting with fear; In the process of easing out of the closet, walking slowly towards her.

Loyalty leaped over the bed, dodging for cover as she crawled rapidly, side-sweeping my leg, making me lose balance and control of the gun.

She lunged over me for the gun, cocked it back, and prepared to shoot my bitch ass until we both saw something from our peripheral that redirected our attention instead of the task at hand. Loyalty backflipped and did a double take.

"Lo!!!No!!! Don't do this." Quita screamed to snap Loyalty out of her deadly trance." Give me the gun Loyalty. She is not worth it." Quita continued to plead.

"Nah, Quita, this bitch took everything from me. I struggle to sleep every night because I'm scared someone is going to creep into my bed and have their way with me. I wake up in cold sweats from bad dreams. Sometimes I even urinate on myself from worry alone. I've slept with people my grandfather's age to convince my mother to love me." Loyalty vented, keeping her aim steady on my head. I slowly crawled to a corner of the room in trembles.

Quita grabbed Loyalty's face to eye level with hers before speaking "It's okay Lo. I love you to the moon and back. You are my sister and I care. I give a fuck." Quita confessed, discreetly grabbing control of the gun and tossing it in the bathroom. Quita hugged and embraced Loyalty.

The sight of all this emotion made my stomach to turn. Loyalty showed me a side of her that I didn't even think she had in her. I also wanted to know how the hell Quita got into my house, but I was grateful because had she not, then I was going to be a goner, for certain.

My balls were slowly but surely coming back because the gun was out of sight "Get out of my house, and never come back." I said.

"With pleasure." Loyalty answered, walking to the door behind Quita but not before she gathered all of her mouth's contents and spit in my face.

Quita snatched Loyalty's hand and guided them to Loyalty's room to gather her things.

## Loyalty

"Don't worry about a thing. You can come and stay with me. We have more than enough room. I will always have your back." Quita said, sincerely as she watched me practically throw everything I had into my suitcase.

So many questions imposed in my head that I needed to think about but getting the hell out of here was step one for me. I could not believe that I was about to lose the only person I've known since birth. This was so surreal to me.  On one note, I was glad to start this new unwritten chapter with my new baby but, unfortunately, Sherry wouldn't be there to witness it. Eventually, I was going to have to come up with a plan for my party of two because I couldn't bear raising my child in someone else's house.

"What will I do, when I leave here since Sherry is all that I know?" I asked Quita, feeling helpless.

"Live, Loyalty, Live." Quita answered.

# CHAPTER 8

*"If he is a real nigga, he will be there for you regardless!" - Quita*

## LOYALTY

3 days later

Tears cascaded down my face angelically as I exposed all my dirty laundry from my skeleton-filled closet to Ms. Jeanette Smalls, Quita's mother. This was so healing for me because this was my first time ever expressing how I felt. Quita was somewhere in her room laying down. That girl could sleep all day if you let her.

"Why couldn't Ms. Smalls be my mother?" I thought to myself, checking out of our intervention momentarily.

Ms. Smalls was so beautiful to me standing at 5'4, 160 lbs. in her zebra-patterned scrubs and long gray locks that graced the crown of her head. She was the perfect example of what a perfect mother should look like to me. She honestly made "50" look like the new "30". I know why she made being a midwife her occupation as she truly made this world a better place.

"You will never have to go back there again, if I have anything to do with it." Ms. Smalls stated matter-of-factly with her hands planted on her hips and disgust written all over her face with every story I revealed." "Never!" she emphasized.

"If Quita didn't show up when she did, I'd probably be on the first flight to prison, and Quita would be planning Sherry's funeral if there was anything left to bury," I said, unremorseful.

Ms. Smalls exhaled, "I'm glad she showed up too because only the Lord knows what will happen when a Lioness is wounded."

I smiled, admiring her comparison of me to a lion. It was during that moment that I realized I was no longer a victim, but a survivor at best. These three days of living without Sherry wasn't so scary after all. She didn't have enough money in her pocket to make me come back.

"How are you really holding up baby?" Ms. Smalls asked, genuinely concerned.

"I'm holding up well. I'm just taking it day by day. I will not allow this one thing get me down. This is just a new beginning for me that I'm rapidly adjusting to." I said, giving the most honest answer that I could for now. Even though I didn't even believe a word of it.

Ms. Smalls looked mighty weird as she shuffled around her bra in the middle of talking to me for something. "This is your key. Make yourself at home. If you need anything, let me or Quita know." Ms. Smalls smiled, placing a gold key in my hand.

"Yes Ma'am, I will." I said, hanging my head low while grabbing the key tightly against my palm.

Ms. Smalls lifted my chin to hers. "Keep your head up baby. Also, let Quita know that I will be in late tonight from work, but that we will still meet for breakfast together in the morning." Ms. Smalls requested, getting up from her seat and heading for the door.

"Mama gone?" Quita asked, rubbing the cold out of her eyes. I don't even think she realized how spooked I was for her scaring the living daylights out of me.

"Uh, yes. She just left." I replied, relaying each message that I was told, getting sleepy myself.

"Hey Qui?" I called, stopping her path towards the bathroom.

"Yeah?" she inquired, turning around and speaking hoarsely

"How did you know Sherry and I were fighting?" I asked, furrowing my brows.

"Your butt dialed me and all I could hear was yelling and screaming, so, I ran to your house, grabbed the spare key under the mat, and let myself in," Quita answered.

I snickered. "It's a blessing you came when you did because Sherry was about to be ***DOA***!" We laughed in unison.

Quita abruptly stopped laughing as her facial expression grew serious "In all the years I've known you, I have never seen you that angry. What in the world would cause you to pull a knife or a smoking gun on your mother?" Quita asked seriously.

I took my time replying to Quita's question to find a rehearsed answer but came up empty. It was just simply better to keep it real and hope she didn't judge me after the fact. "When you find out you are pregnant by some random man in the street, and you don't have any idea who can possibly be the father. No to mention that she orchestrated the whole thing and has been selling my body for money. I feel damn right bamboozled." I confessed.

Quita gasped in shock and at a loss for words. "How far long are you, and are you going to keep it?" Quita bombarded me with questions, recklessly picking my mind. Then, all those images that I was attempting to put behind me began invading my mind.

"In my mind, I want to abort it because the child will never know who its dad is which will make the child a bastard, but in my heart, I feel like this baby will be my chance at redemption. I will give the child the love that I seek in others, and in return, they will give me that unconditional love a child gives regardless of who you are or what you've done. Oh… and I am 2 months." I told her, pulling up my shirt.

Quita nodded, with her finger under her chin in deep thought as she stared at my protruding belly. "How come you have never told me any of this as long as we've been friends?" Quita was seemingly hurt.

I held my head down. "Well, what was I supposed to say? I'm a prostitute and my mother is my pimp. I don't know, Qui, I just felt like in my own little way, I was simply fighting for my mother's love and a place in her cold heart. Please don't judge me. It was the only ultimatum I was given besides getting put out. She left me no other choice. I guess I was just green that it was only supreme manipulation." I begged and pleaded through tears.

Quita got up to console me, grasping my emotional ass, as tears clouded her own vision. "I am your sister through anything. I am here for you, but don't make permanent decisions in temporary emotional states." She told me.

I understood exactly what she meant. Deep down inside, I knew my life was about to change forever in seven months. I had to prepare to be the best mother that I could, even if it resulted in losing Ramirez. He either had to take this two-for-one special or nothing at all.

We laid there for hours, rocking each other back and forth before getting ready for bed. No words had to be spoken because we understood one another.

"Qui?" I tapped Quita on her shoulder before she drifted off into a deep slumber.

"Yes?" she answered drowsily, opening her eyes while laying on her favor-ite pillow.

"Do you think I spoiled my chances with Ramirez?" I asked curiously.

Quita turned on her back and refocused her gaze on me. "If he is a real nigga, he will be there for you regardless. We don't chase, we replace. Long as I have breath in my body, he or she will be taken care of. Now, goodnight! "She answered with finality.

I laid on my pillow smiling as every chip on my shoulder was slowly beginning to fall off.

The next day

"Get up, Loyalty! I want to cook breakfast for mama, I need to go to the store." Quita panted, shaking me out of my sleep.

I hadn't rested until the wee hours of the night. I even felt better after praying the entire dawn for peace in my heart and soul. Finally, it seemed like my prayers were being answered. It was the first day since leaving Sherry's house that I didn't wake up, crying.

What time is it heifer?" I asked her groggily.

"Time for you to get your ass up, and come on," she commanded, giving me a piece of her blunt.

"Aww, okay. I'm coming." I groaned, relieving myself from the bed. I headed for the bathroom to take care of my hygiene.

We drove in silence on our way to the store until we made it into Walmart's parking lot and grabbed our buggy.

"Is waffles, eggs, and bacon okay with you?" Quita asked.

"Yeah," I answered sleepily.

I picked up a People magazine from the newsstand that stood in front of me that had another Beyoncé & Jay-Z cheating scandal on the cover, which happened to be my favorite iconic Hollywood couple. I followed Quita down every aisle she went on without ever missing a beat. I dropped the magazine suddenly when I felt a pair of eyes burning a hole into me but when I turned around and saw no one, I continued following Quita again until she found the shortest line to ring up her things.

"Does that magazine have anything to do with you and I being together?" Ramirez flirted, giving me that devilish smirk.

My eyes shot up from the first word that left his tonsils and traveled to my brain. "Maybe, Maybe not." I flirted back. "In all the times I have been to this store, I did not know you worked here."

"There are a lot of things you don't know about me, beautiful, since you have been ignoring me around school because of the incident at the party. He said, making me feel all types of guilt.

I couldn't deny the fact that he was right. I twiddled my thumbs repeatedly because I was too embarrassed to respond at that second.

"Uhh… Hmmm." A short, gray-haired elderly lady grunted behind Quita and I.

"Do you need a throat laxative or something?" Quita snapped at the elderly lady with a menacing stare. The elderly lady just looked at her like she was scum of the earth and scrunched up her face. "I didn't think so." Quita taunted.

I looked at Ramirez with puppy dog eyes. "I'm sorry. Okay? I guess I was just kind of ashamed of the whole ordeal. You know?" I pleaded, hoping he understood where I was coming from and accept my honest apology.

"You have nothing to be ashamed of baby girl. On another note, what do I have to do to gain a date with you?" He inquired, returning my puppy face.

I blushed and exhaled. I decided to put my pride to the side and go after what I wanted.

"You can start by jotting down my number which is 678-272-8305, but don't call me collect." I laughed, revealing my pearly whites.

"Bet. I'll see you later gorgeous." He licked his lips.

"Well let me get out of here before grandma loses her girdle." Quita chimed in. We all laughed together.

The lady cleared her throat again, ignoring Quita's threats.

"See you later, my lady," Ramirez said.

"After a while, crocodile." I returned.

Chrisette Michele's "Let Me Win" resounded throughout Quita's house as I cleaned up for Ms. Smalls to make my stay at her home as easy as possible. I wanted to earn my keeps somehow. Hell, I did it for Sherry when she barely fed me, so I thought it was the least I could do.

"Breakfast is served," Quita announced." Let your girl know what you think."

My mouth salivated at the sight before me. Waffles, scrambled eggs, and fresh crispy bacon sat neatly on the plate with a cup of orange juice by the side. I couldn't wait to dig in after prayer.

"Thanks sis," I told her.

"Thanks baby. This is delicious." Ms. Smalls stated with a mouth full of food.

"You all are welcome, but you know a Sista can burn." Quita praised herself. After devouring our food as a family, I took everyone's plates and began to wash the dishes.

"Hey girls, I am about to go lie down. I will prepare dinner after my nap," Ms. Smalls retorted while walking in the direction of her bedroom. As soon as Ms. Smalls was out of earshot, Quita started her analysis of me.

"Someone is feeling a certain someone." Quita teased.

"Who? Ramirez?" I questioned.

"Yep," Quita answered.

"Girl please, I barely know the man."

"But you want to though," Quita stated in a matter-of-fact tone.

"Maybe I do," I whispered.

"She only been here for two weeks, came here with her girls, but she trying to leave with me." Trey Songz "Foreign" echoed from my phone, signaling an incoming call. I picked up my phone, but I didn't recognize the number. I answered anyway.

"Hello?" I said.

"What are you doing?" Ramirez inquired. I had finally gotten used to hearing his voice.

"Lying across the bed. You?" She questioned back.

"Kicking shit, I just got off."

"Oh cool," I said, not trying to sound desperate.

"Beautiful, would you like to go out with me tonight?" he asked.

I paused for a few seconds, so I wouldn't sound too enthused. "Sure. Where, are we going?"

"It's a surprise. You just be ready by eight, my lady." He demanded and hung up the phone.

I screamed at the top of my lungs, "Yes, Yes, Yes," until I remembered that Ms. Smalls was asleep. I woke Quita out of her sleep to help me decide what to wear.

Then, I said a silent prayer: "God, I have been through so much. Please allow Ramirez be the breakthrough for my heart and not the breakdown to my soul."

# CHAPTER 9

*"You are bad bitch; don't you ever die - Loyalty*

## LOYALTY

Ding! Dong! The doorbell rang, but I already knew who was at the door.

"Qui, can you get that for me?" I asked, putting the finishing touches to my makeup in the zebra decorated bathroom.

"Yeah, I guess." She answered, removing herself from the lid of the toilet seat.

"You are a bad bitch; Don't you ever die!" I told myself. Adorning a beautiful BCBG cutout dress, diamond-crusted hoops, and some black Manolo pumps with a dash of red lipstick. Once I was satisfied with my appearance, I grabbed my jacket and headed for the door.

"Where are you taking my sister, Sanchez?" Quita interrogated with her arms crossing her chest.

"None of your business Mamacita." He smirked.

"You can smile all you want, but whatever you do to her, I'm going to do to you." Quita shot back, returning his infamous smirk.

"I got her. I promise." He said, placing his hands up as if he was ready to be arrested.

"Quita, what are you doing to my date?" I said, intervening between the two.

"Nothing, just protecting what's mine." Quita defended her stance.

"Thanks chick, you always have my back." We did our famous handshake and kissed each other's cheek.

"Well kids, you all have fun, and don't do anything I wouldn't do." Quita said, pushing us outside and screaming "Bad bitches never die." Before closing the door.

## Ramirez

"We're here!" I announced, removing Loyalty's blindfold from her eyes. She glanced out the window and stretched her eyes open at the sight of the juke joint, but I hoped she trusted me enough not to bring her anywhere that would potentially put her in danger. I killed the engine and got out of the car to open the door for her like the gentleman I was.

"You're looking mighty dapper tonight." She complimented me. I stood in a black blazer, white button-down polo shirt, black slacks, and some suede Chuck Taylor's. I grabbed her hand, kissed the top of it, and slowly walked her to the door. I got so excited when I noticed her face finally relax and even smiled once we made it inside. I'm glad she had a change of heart. I loved this place for dates because the low lights that illuminated the building gave it an intimate feel.

"You look great tonight Loyalty. "I said for the thousandth time as we were being seated. Loyalty kept her mouth gaped open like she still was shocked because we were on a date.

"How did you find this place? I've never been in this area before," she asked seriously, fixing the tussles in her hair.

"This is where I come to clear my head and let go of my pain," I answered without much detail. She nodded confusingly.

"How you'll doing tonight?" The MC of the night asked in an exciting tone.

"Good." We all screamed in unison. "Well, tonight is Open-Mic night, where we reveal our struggles, wars, and battles that lives in our hearts. Don't leave this building without letting it all out. Do we have any volunteers? He announced, inviting the audience to the stage. I instantly stood to Loyalty's astonishment.

"Well come on then." The host invited me to the stage.

"Keep my seat warm for me beautiful," I said and walked to the front of the building. Loyalty smiled.

"What's your name son?" The host asked me.

"Ramirez Sanchez." He stated in the microphone.

"Well, there you have it, folks, let's give Ramirez a round of applause." The Mc said before giving me the mic. I swallowed nervously because this was the first time I performed in front of a date.

"This one is for you, my lady."

*"Let Me Win"*
*This game is like a gamble*
*Here's my heart to handle*
*Need you to be gentle*
*You should let me win*
*I'm not your heart of playing*
*Don't know what to say*
*I'm tryna catch a break*
*You should let me win*

I sang a cover of Chrisette's new joint with emotion, conviction, and revelation that earned me a standing ovation and a round of applause. Loyalty looked on in amazement at the purity and lyrics of my voice which stirred up emotions I didn't know was there. There was not a dry eye in sight including my own.

"Why didn't you tell me you can sing………..? Not to mention, that is one of my favorite songs." Loyalty sang drunkenly.

"Well, it's something I keep hidden because I'm known for being this basketball god when all I really want to do is sit in the corner with my guitar and sing my heart out." I replied with certainty.

"Is this the only time you sing?" She asked.

"Yes, and when I put flowers on my mother's grave." I frowned.

"How did she die?"

"Giving birth to me," I answered solemnly, hoping she just changed the subject before my anxiety got the best of me.

## Loyalty

I silently wondered what it would be like to have a mother's love that would sacrifice her own life to give a child a life of their own. I noticed his saddened demeanor and wiped the lone tear that left from his eye.

"Are you okay?" I whispered. He nodded.

I grabbed his face, lifted his chin and pulled him in for a long passionate kiss. "So, Loyalty, are you going to let me be the winner of your heart?" He excitedly asked.

"If you can heal my pain, wipe my tears, and remain loyal, then, you can share my life." I answered honestly. I was in no state of mind to deal with anyone's nonsense.

"I had a nice time with you tonight Casanova." I lightly chuckled at his new nickname. He walked me to my car with his jacket around my shoulders.

"Likewise, my lady, when will I see you again?" He faced me and stared.

"Whenever you would like to. I'm here at your disposal." I answered by kissing him on the lips passionately.

I have never had a boyfriend before. All those girls at school and yet, he chose me. I must admit it truly felt good to have someone who took such an interest in me. I guess I was just going to see how this goes because I surely wasn't going to get my hopes up just yet.

# CHAPTER 10

*"You don't miss me. You miss me for what I use to do for you!*
*- Loyalty*

## LOYALTY

3 months later

"Ms. Daniels, you will be having a healthy baby girl in roughly four months. Are you still considering keeping the little lily after giving birth?" Dr. Penelli asked me with a concerned expression applied on his face, but he abruptly halted my answer when his eyes shifted from me to my ultrasound monitors as one of the machines began beeping rapidly and I wondered why because I felt fine.

"I wouldn't have it any other way. This is my chance to start anew;" I answered happily, after giving Quita the ultrasound pictures. Quita smiled and began making baby noises at the little person in the picture. I knew that I already had the best aunt that money can buy.

"That is wonderful to hear as I feel you will be an excellent mother, but I am concerned about you after viewing your stress test. Have you been under any stress that will prevent you from having a healthy pregnancy journey? I do not want to put you on immediate bed rest, but I will if your lifestyle will harm your daughter." Dr. Penelli warned.

"There was a minor setback, but I have everything under control," I assured him in a definite tone.

It wasn't until he said, daughter, that the realization came that I of all people was getting ready to be a mother. Words couldn't explain how afraid I truly was.

Dr. Penelli nodded apprehensively.

"Okay… The only way you will be able to carry this baby full term is to eat healthy, avoid any stress, and take good care of yourself. I'm going to also schedule a mandatory appointment at the beginning of next month to check your stats and stress levels." He scolded before walking out of the room and allowing me to get dressed.

I sat quietly for a minute after hearing Dr. Penelli's request and warnings. At that moment, I knew I had to change my life around to keep any danger from my embryo. I had always imagined Sherry being here holding my hand through this entire process, but if she came anywhere near me during this present time, I will kill her.

Quita got up and helped me down from the check-up bed. "Lo, I'm very proud of you. Most folks can't handle what you've been through. It takes great courage to carry a child when they are conceived from a very dark place and situation." Quita admitted to me wholeheartedly.

"Thank you so much. I can't take away what has been given to me. It brings me joy when she kicks, sleeps, or tumbles. I just want someone to love me unconditionally as your mother does you. I want someone to look at me like the greatest and strongest human being they have ever seen." I said, hoping that Quita bought the one-sided story I was selling to her.

On the inside, I was very afraid and wondered what was to become of my future. I even wondered 'Will my baby girl love me for who I am or resent me like Sherry? In some weird way, I missed Sherry. Before Quita entered my life, Sherry was all that I knew, and I silently prayed that she was okay, but I just couldn't fathom one more moment of escorting.

"Do you have a name for her yet?" Quita asked.

"Yes, Justice Messiah Daniels." I happily announced, smiling.

"I like! Come on, before we miss Ramirez's game." Quita said, gunning for the car.

"Let's Go, Rebels! Let's Go!" The Lady Rebels cheered for our men's basketball team as we assisted them by screaming across the floor at their competition, The Lady Hornets."

"This is a good game, Lo, and Ya' boy is doing numbers," Quita said to me during one of her cheer breaks.

I silently nodded like I had heard her, but I was too focused on the game. It was Ramirez's championship game before graduation. I knew a "W" would mean the world to him. It was the 4th quarter and we only had 20 seconds left. We were only behind a point."10,9,8,7,6,5,4,3,2…."

The crowd roared ferociously.

Ramirez appeared to be sneaking to the other end of the court to sneak for a dunk. He dribbled with precision until he reached the basket and dunked while one of the defensive players held on to his legs, attempting to stop him.

He scored before the buzzer alarm ringed.

"Yawl, Yawl, look at my dab," Ramirez said along with his team as everyone danced and sang in happiness. The entire team grabbed Ramirez and lifted him upon their shoulders as they traveled to the locker room to freshen up. The crowd went haywire. It was Ramirez's fourth championship win.

"Come on Quita, I want to meet him at the door as soon as he comes out of the locker room," I exclaimed. I was beaming with excitement.

"Good Game, baby. You busted your ass tonight." I praised Ramirez before giving him a bear hug which resulted in a hot sweaty kiss.

"Thanks bae. You are my good luck charm." Ramirez said, in-between shaking everyone's hands while sweat protruded from his skin. He stopped in midstride as something peculiar caught his eyes causing him to choke on his tears.

"What are you doing here papa? I thought you hated me." Ramirez said to his father.

"Mijo, I don't hate you. It just took me a long time to finally accept Gina's passing. I lov…..e you more than you realize." Hector stuttered, breaking down in tears of his own. He grabbed and hugged Ramirez for the first time in his whole life. "Give me a chance to make it right and if I can't, I'll try forever." He continued.

"I love you too," Ramirez replied.

Nothing in this world could replace this special moment for him. This moment is what he dreamed of. I silently hoped that this transition from Hector wasn't temporary. Quita and I looked on in awe at the sight of father and son uniting, and each wished we had a dad of our own. Ramirez turned around and motioned for me to come here.

"This right here is the special lady in my life, Ms. Loyalty Daniels," Ramirez said with his hand around my shoulder to Hector. We shook hands slowly, sizing each other up.

"Nice to meet you, young lady. You seemed to have changed this knuckle-head for the better. He is much happier now!" Hector smiled.

"Likewise, sir. I've heard a lot about you." I told him.

"Good things? I hope." He replied.

"Well, sometimes," I admitted as we shared a light chuckle.

"Loyaltyyyyyyyyyyyyyy!!!!" I heard a woman who sounded just like my mother screaming my name at a far distance, walking swiftly in our direction. As she approached closer, it confirmed my suspicion. It was none other than the one and only, Sherry Daniels. I inhaled and ex-haled repeatedly for the wrath to come. If I had to dust her off on sight, then, so be it, pregnant and all. Quita instantly stood in a fighting stance, down for whatever.

"Baby, Mama miss you! I'm ready for you to come on home. I won't hurt you anymore." Sherry pleaded, gasping for air. Sherry looked a lot differ-ent from our last encounter three months ago, she had lost a lot of weight. Her hair was straggly, and she seemed to be "higher" beyond recognition. This plea appeared to be a cry for help if anything?

I shook my head in disgust. "You don't miss me. You miss me for what I use to do for you, but I'm sorry Mama, I can't do that for you anymore." I refused to cry or mess up my makeup over an imbecile of a mother.

"Please, Loyalty, one more time. I have an eviction notice on my window-sill, and I haven't eaten in days. If you do this last favor for me, I will love you forever and never bother you again." Sherry weakly replied.

"No more! No more! No more!" I screamed over the crowd, clenching my fist. Instantly, bringing the crowd's attention towards the both of us.

Hector touched the back of Sherry's shoulder to grab her attention from the beat down that was about to occur. "Wait, did you ever go by the name "Ashley"?" He asked, furrowing his eyebrows to focus on her body language for any sense of lies.

Sherry stood frozen, carefully examining the man before her. "Yes, over fifteen years ago, but what's it to you?" Sherry scrunched up her face in annoyance with Hector, interrupting her pleas with me.

"Do you remember me? Hector Sanchez?" Hector searched Sherry's face.

"Yes, I do. The man that stole my heart and has never given it back." Sherry covered her mouth in awe.

"Papa, how do you know this lady?" Curiosity must've gotten the best of Ramirez too because I swear this was some crazy shit.

"How did our parents already know each other? This was some young and the restless shit." I thought to myself.

"This is Gina's best friend. "Ashley" or "Sherry" is the woman your mother spoke about in her letter to you," Hector confessed with sympathy.

Quita, and I all looked confused and appalled, but we knew that the letter meant nothing good by the scowl etched across Ramirez's angry face. Before any of us had a chance to react, Ramirez ran up on Hector, cocked his elbow back and punched him in the jaw with tears of anger streaming down his face until he sped out of the gym full speed. Hector fell to the ground off impact alone. At that moment, I felt embarrassed, ashamed, and low. I despised my mother with a straight passion.

"Damn! Damn! Damn! Sherry." I yelled in frustration before turning on my heels in search for Ramirez. The rain did nothing but cloud my vision as I looked around seeing nothing out of the ordinary except a group of guys on the bus ramp shooting dice. "Hey Fellas, did yawl see what way Sanchez went?" I asked them.

All of them pointed in the same direction of his car. I attempted to sprint to his car to catch him before he peeled off, but it was too late. In horror, I watched as his car sped off out of the school zone at over 100 miles.

"Damn," I said to no one. Thinking quickly on my feet, I remembered that I still had Quita's keys in my purse.

Jumping in her car with no time to waste, I pressed the gas as hard as I could. Hopefully without alarming him of my presence but that plan halted when he stopped the car abruptly and threw himself out. I immediately followed suit, barefooted.

"Ramirez, what are you doing?" I panicked.

"I'm fucking jumping." He answered.

"Why?"

"The pain of losing my mother is too much for me to bear anymore. Why would she leave me here with a man that wants nothing to do with me? I'm tired of this shiittt......." He screamed, hysterically.

As he kept pacing the plank on the bridge, my mind was having a tug of war of my own: Should I leave him here alone to annihilate himself or rescue him like he did for me not long ago? I had no idea what to do or say to get him down. It seemed to me like his mind was already made up. I didn't even have a chance to answer myself because of the piercing scream that erupted in my ears. Ramirez tripped over the ledge and was dangling off the edge. I peered off the railing and saw only three of his fingers, barely hanging on.

"I love you, Ramirez, I swear I do. Don't do this! You are my sunshine and light. Without you here, life just won't be right. I didn't know what love was until I met you. Please, let me help you!" I pleaded with the little breath I had left, while, extending my hand out for him to grab it. The rain showers were increasing by the second and I knew his hands were getting more slippery. It was becoming difficult for me to see through my glasses in the mist.

"Loyaltyyyyyyy…" he screamed, reaching for my hand. I cried profusely. My tears and the rain were just not mixing at the moment.

"Give me your hand," I demanded.

Ramirez struggled hard to give me his other hand to pull him up. He was holding on with all his might. "I love you too." He weakly admitted like he was giving up. I snatched my glasses off and threw them somewhere before I squinted my eyes to focus.

"Not on my watch. We got this." I said to encourage him while extending my arm out as far as I could before I slowly grabbed his body and slung it across my back to pull him up like Pumbaa carried Simba in Lion's King. The minute I brought him from over the ledge, he collapsed. I could hear the ambulance not far away from where we were.

"God, I know you didn't answer my prayers about Sherry and I promised myself I would be patient until you carried my troubles away, but if you can hear me, please allow Ramirez to make it through. I'm already okay if you're already done with me." I prayed to the "Most-High" as the paramedics arrived.

## Ramirez

I awoke to the sounds of the hospital monitors buzzing in my ears. I was confused, how the hell did I end up here and why was I so damn groggy?

The pain that erupted from my body felt like someone had set me on fire.

"Glad to see you up for a change." Loyalty joked, beside me with excitement.

Things were becoming even weirder for me because I didn't expect to see her here out of all people. Though, I was happy to see her because she always seemed to bring out the best of me when she was around. I honestly couldn't imagine life without her in it. Butterflies suddenly replaced all the anxiety I was feeling presently until I jumped up after noticing all the cords connected in me.

"How long have I been here?" I asked her.

"Three Days." She answered.

Her answer caused my mind to go into overdrive without responding as I thought about anything that would jog my memory but came up empty. With my pride set aside, I decided to ask, even if it made me look crazy.

" You don't remember anything, Do you?" She asked me. I shook my head.

"How? When? Where? Why?" I asked, never completing a whole sentence. She giggled.

"Well," she paused." Basically, your father delivered a low blow that caused you to run out of the school, jump in your car, and try to commit suicide until I saved you from falling over the ledge." Loyalty explained. I saw her cross her fingers behind her back which meant she had to be intentionally leaving parts out of the real story. Little by little, my memory was slowly coming back to me. 'Knock, Knock,' someone knocked on my hospital door, interrupting my thoughts from running wild.

"Come in," I said, patting my hair down and wiping the crust from the corners of my mouth.

Hector walked in with a bouquet of yellow roses, and my favorite teddy bear from my bedroom at home which instantly reminded me of my mother. He kept everything on the table but remained silent as if something was drastically bothering him. It took him exactly two minutes before deciding to speak.

"How are you guys doing?" Hector asked, fake smiling at Loyalty

"Fine, Mr. Sanchez." She answered.

"Straight," I replied.

"You mind if I have a word with Ramirez?" Hector asked. Loyalty obliged and walked out of the room. Hector placed his hands in his deep pocket, contemplating his approach with me this time. Everything came racing back to me at once.

Hector gulped hard as if he was swallowing a pill. "Ramirez, I struggled hard growing up because I was always trying to be the man of the streets. I battled being a follower or a leader daily. I wanted to be there for my family. I really did. It just took me too long to recognize what I had back home. I know I don't deserve your sympathy, but, allow me to try to make it right. If I could take it back, I would, but I can't." Hector mercifully pleaded with his tone and body language. I cut my eyes with a quickness, ignoring Hector's heartfelt apology.

"Negro, please. You can't take shit back because she is dead as a doorknob. Get the fuck out my face. You are the sorriest nigger I've ever seen. I don't want to see, hear, or even feel you. You're nothing but a sack of cowardly blood. I hate your fucking guts so dismiss yourself!" I hoped the morphine in my IV from the button that I pushed took effect. Hector held his head down in defeat.

"As you wish, Hijo, if you ever find it in your heart to forgive me or at least try, I will forever be indebted to you, but these gifts are for you."

Adhering to my request, Hector walked out of the room, running into Loyalty simultaneously who was listening at the door, speechless. Loyalty tip-toed back inside to feel the vibe of the scene but, she knew it didn't go well by the scowl on my face.

"Do you want to talk about it boo?" Loyalty cheerfully asked me.

Although, she looked hesitant to speak. Often, I knew she thought it was crazy that she was able to be there for someone when her own life was in shambles daily.

"I hate him, I hate him, I hate him. He has never been there for me. I had to raise myself alone when all I wanted was a father. I needed a father." Ramirez muffled in a daze, throwing the teddy bear across the room.

## Loyalty

When I saw the tears escape down Ramirez's pretty boy face, I held my head down. I felt so damaged on the inside that there was no possible way I could help someone else, but here I was in the presence of a man that took my entire breath away just by the way he called my name. It was just the way he looked at me. Not like some helpless charity case but like a woman in my own unique way. He didn't judge me by the clothes that I wore or that my glasses were crooked. I could tell by the way he treated me that he had what I yearned for and vice-versa

"Everything is going to be okay." I kept chanting until I truly believed those words myself.

After deciding to stay with him, I caressed his cheek and allowed him to vent all night long until he fell into a deep slumber in the middle of him telling me something horrible about Hector. Secretly, I was glad Ramirez fell asleep because I needed some time to think and digest everything he told me. I kissed his lips and said a silent prayer over him before traveling to the window to watch the nightfall. 'Exhausted' was an understatement for me. I pulled the curtains back and stared at the moon and stars. I reflected on my past, present, and even, my future. I reflected on my life, how it did an entire "180" in a matter of five months. How did I go from being invisible to a prostitute to a single mother, all in a matter of five months?

My knees started buckling by the way the baby was swimming in my stomach. The clothes I wore kept my secret at bay. My bulge was still barely noticeable. I hoped Ramirez wouldn't leave me when shit did hit the fan, but at this point, I was prepared for whatever, even the ultimate worst. It just would hurt me like hell because he completed me and we both seemed to know loss and heartbreak better than anyone.

To me, it just seemed like Ramirez just fell out of the sky and gave me the love I longed for. I truly couldn't imagine anything standing in our way of being together. But with the life I lived, who knows? Even though our union seemed effortless and priceless. In life, there was no manual; I had to take everything in stride and know that everyone didn't think or feel the same. If Ramirez did decide to call it quits, then, I would just have to cherish every moment we ever spent together and walk away. Besides, I had a baby that depended on my next breath and that was enough for me. My favorite motto in life was F.E.A.R. (Face Everything and Rise) which meant what's going to be, will be, anyway. That was the motto that got me through my worst days.

After sending my mind into overkill about the possibilities of Ramirez finding out how I use to sell my body for money, I walked lazily back to my hospital recliner, snuggled up and tuned the TV to 'Martin' before drifting off to sleep.

# CHAPTER 11

*Hey, it must be the Moneayyyyy!!- Shay*

## SHERRY

I asked Shay to come over to help me find the life insurance policy that Hector got for me, many years ago, there was no telling where it could be. Hell, I could've used it as a place to hold my cocaine. At least, I hoped not. In the line of crack heads, there was no limit to getting high because all resources had to be utilized.

I jumped at the announcement of the door being opened without my consent, but I forgot about the spare key that Shay had in case of emergencies and this definitely was one.

"Hey, it must be the Moneayyyyy!!" Shay screamed, walking through the door, looking like a yeast infected person with her too tight pink booty shorts and camisole when she knew she was a full-fledged "BBW" in every sense of the word. I hoped she didn't think she looked like "Moneayyyyy" because "Unctie" will be more like it. But if she liked it, I loved it.

"Girl don't come in here with all that damn noise. I am trying to concentrate." I scolded.

Shay looked at me sideways with disgust." How can you con-cen-trate looking like shit? Oh, I know why you can't concentrate because it's too much air going across that big ass head." She joked.

"Oh, Miss baby gap, got jokes today. Do me a favor and stay out of children's place." I snapped back.

I felt the top of my head for my wig which was nowhere to be found. Instantly, I felt flushed and began running up the stairs to get dressed. Who was I without my wig? No one. I couldn't believe I forgot all about "Peaches" (My Wig).

Once I entered the bathroom and fixed myself up, I placed my lace front wig on backward to hide the bald spots I caused when I pulled my hair out, whenever I'm stressed. Satisfied with my looks, I sashayed back downstairs like a contestant in Ru Paul's Drag Race.

"Well, how do I look?" I asked, seductively.

"Like a damn fool, but you will do," Shay clowned. "But, is this what you're looking for? Shay continued, turning serious.

I continued to search through my Adidas shoebox of documents, never really paying Shay any attention because she played too much until I looked up and saw the insurance policy dangling out of her hand.

"OH! MY! GOD!" I screamed like someone was killing me.

Snatching the policy pamphlet out of her hand, I read it with my cataract-infected eyes and started to jump for joy. I grabbed Shay by the arm and danced with her.

"That's my best friend, that's my best friend!" I sang in my Tokyo Vanity voice.

We laughed and played until reality hit me like a ton of bricks as I sat down. The policy clearly stated that I was the second beneficiary after Ramirez who would be the next of kin. I didn't want to kill both of them but as I've already stated, "Getting money was by any means necessary, I didn't give a fuck about a price.

"Girl, you do realize that Hector and Ramirez have to die for you to collect any coins?" Shay asked me.

"Duhhhh, I'm aware. That is why I might need your help," I replied.

Shay saw the murderous look in my eyes and appeared shaken. I don't even know how we maintained a friendship after all these years because she was scary as a fuck. But that was my girl, and I loved her. She has been the only consistent person to show me love besides Loyalty. Speaking of which, I hadn't talked to Loyalty since the basketball game. I missed the little-crooked face bitch. Let's be clear, I miss her making my money. Don't get it twisted.

"Oh, hell no! I'm not helping you with shit. So, X me out of your little plans. I want nothing to do with it. I still have nightmares about your uncles sometimes. Besides, I'm on the way to Tony's house for some good ole' lovin'." Shay said, grabbing her purse.

Tony was an ex Shay could never seem to leave alone. God, I wish he did because he was no good for her with his rat poisoned breath.

"Gone, get, then," I said to play with her as Shay walked out the door.

I closed the door behind her and came up with an entire plan to get all the money owed to me in less than thirty days, starting with Hector.

"I guess Hector didn't realize the side effects of a broken heart. I laid out my clothes and prepared for Phase 1." I thought.

I went over my plans a thousand times to make sure it was foolproof. I really considered being a hitman in my hey-day. Especially how I executed my uncles, but, now, who was going to hire my busted and disgusted ass?

# Hector

I grabbed another beer from my twelve pack of Budweiser before another attempt to watch this Sunday's football game. Even though, I couldn't really enjoy it because so many things plagued my mind.

Desiring to right my wrongs, I turned the game off, sat down at the kitchen table and began writing down some ideas on a sheet of paper to make it up to Ramirez but came up with nothing. I felt like a failure to my wife and only child. The biggest difference between loving a child and having love for a child was the difference between a father and a daddy. It was the strongest fight I dealt with, internally.

" I promised Gina that I would always love, protect, and honor my son but I only ever seemed to hate, resent, and blatantly ignore him. I know Gina is probably turning in her grave, if she knew how things had turned out, for the worst." I thought to myself.

"Ding, Dong!" The doorbell ranged, interrupting my thoughts. I lazily removed myself from the table, wondering, who the hell could be at the door?

" Who is it?" I asked, peeking through the peephole.

"Oh shit! What the hell does she want? I thought.

"The lady of your deadliest memories." The visitor seductively answered. I grimaced at the creepiest recognition of her voice.

"What do you want Sherry?" I frowned upon opening the door.

Sherry leaned her elbow on the side of the door like she was some vixen, in a poorly made red seductress dress and her wig on backward. I'm guessing that was her style.

"What's wrong baby, you're not happy to see me?" She whispered, peeking in.

I just simply stared at the only woman who I have never been able to resist. Sherry's sex appeal alone made me a widow. Sherry use to be a woman in every sense of the word with her glamour and feminism. I thought back to the times when she captured everyone's attention in every room she walked in. I wondered, where did Sherry disappear to after Gina's death? But, I was too consumed with guilt to do any further research.

"Can I come in? Is there anyone here?" She asked me.

"No, and I guess," I answered, solemnly.

I ignored the eerie feeling that clouded my reasoning. Against my better judgment, I let her in. I poured myself a glass of scotch and offered some to Sherry but she declined.

"What can I do for you Sherry?" I asked her, jumping straight to the point.

I was not prepared for anyone's bullshit today. I elevated my feet in my recliner and got prepared for whatever. She sucked her teeth at my forwardness.

"You know what I want and the answer is you. Nothing more, nothing less." She licked her crusty lips and raised her dress above her knees, exposing her bare clitoris. I frowned.

"That ship sailed a long time ago. I got love for you but I'm not in love with you. All we can be is friends." I said in finality.

Sherry deliriously laughed as if I just told the funniest joke she had ever heard.

"Hector, my darling, you were mine then, and you're mine now. In case you won't have me voluntarily, I will see to it that no one else will. On second thought, I think I will have a glass of scotch." She replied, with not even a hint of a smile.

"Sherry, you are crazier than I thought. Didn't you hear me? I'm not into you like that anymore but since we're being so up, close, and personal; what really happened to Gina? Because the doctor said that she delivered a healthy baby boy, and by the time they returned, Gina was dead without a reasonable cause." I said, folding my arms across my chest, demanding an answer.

## SHERRY

"I told you once, and I tell you again, if I can't have you, then, nobody else will," I responded as Hector got up to retrieve my drink.

17 years ago

Shay only called when she had the "Tea", so, I had hoped this was one of those calls because I needed a "pick-me-up" as I answered the phone on the second ring.

"Bittttchhhh, you know Gina, bald-headed ass just had that baby." Shay sang in the phone. I smiled. This was better than any piece of seafood. I knew Hector wasn't there because he had just climbed from out of me.

I was in Garden City on the other side of town to pick up some seafood from Jackie's but made a quick U-turn upon hearing the news about my nemesis. My best friend always came through with the news.

"Oh yeah? What room number is she in?" I said, concerned.

"Why?" Shay asked, confusingly.

"Because I want to buy her some flowers and a get-well card. Bitch just give me the damn room number." I answered, killing the good girl act.

"435! Damn!" "Child bye! You must not remember who the fuck you talking to? You don't have a nice bone in your fucking body. So, tell me what's really good?" Shay said, dismissing the bullshit I was spitting.

"Can't get anything past you," I joked with extreme sarcasm. "But I'm going up there to let that bitch know that Hector is mine and only mine. I'm also going to tell her to take that bastard baby, run away, and never resurface." I continued.

"And if she doesn't?" Shay countered.

"Come on, Shay. There is no such thing as telling me no. You, out of all people should know that. She will either take heed or get dealt with, accordingly." I replied, nonchalantly.

"Girl, you are one crazy ass bitch."

"And you know this, but I'm going to call you back. I'm about to get dressed." I lied.

I hung up the phone to get out of the car at the hospital. As I approached the receptionist desk, I applied the fakest smile that I could muster

"May I help you?" The frail white woman asked me.

"Why yes, what room number is Gina's Sanchez in?" I said in my white-professional voice.

"Are you family?" She inquired.

"Yes, I am. I am her sister." The receptionist looked skeptically at me. I hoped my smile didn't look plastered. She appeared ready to get off, so, I'm sure she didn't care.

"Oh ok. She's in room 445." The lady answered, scanning the clipboard.

"Thanks." I turned to the elevator and pressed the fourth floor after I got in.

"That ole lying ass bitch. But, the show must go on." I thought, thinking about Shay's false information.

After reaching the fourth floor, I had one goal in mind: to fight or kill for my man. The black, pimple-faced CNA seemed to be bringing a tray to Gina's room until I stopped her in her tracks.

"Excuse me. Is that food for Ms. Waters?" Sherry glanced at her name tag.

"Yes, and you are?" The lady asked with attitude written on her face. She appeared to hate her job, but I was going to make her one patient less, if necessary.

"Ms. Lucky, is it? I am her sister and I will bring her the tray. I wanted to surprise her." I replied, glancing at her identification badge.

"How sweet?" Ms. Lucky mocked and walked away.

" If I had a little more time, I would've beaten that bitch's ass for her smart-ass remarks," I said out loud to no one.

I walked in to a sleeping Gina and thought this was "perfect." I sat the tray down in front of her. Discreetly, I unhooked her IV bag and poked a hole into it before injecting methyl chloride inside of it and placed it back where it belonged.

"The poison should kill her in less than 30 minutes. But I decided to mix it in her food for good measure." I thought as I opened the top of the tray and poured the entire bottle into Gina's mash potatoes and Salisbury steak, mixed it, and carefully placed it back. Walking to the side of Gina's bed, I slapped the fire from her angelic face.

"Get up bitch," I demanded. Gina jumped up out of her slumber like she was scared for her dear life. Well, as she should be.

"Who are you? What do you want? Gina said, holding her face in pain.

"Look! Who I am doesn't matter but I'm only going to tell you this, once. The man you're in love with is mine from the soles of his feet. So, I'm going to give you two choices. One, you give Hector up, take the kid, and leave town or two, you can die now with a broken heart and leave behind a boyfriend and bastard baby. The choice is yours because, truthfully, I don't give a fuck. However, you want to play it, he is coming home to me regardless." I tapped my freshly French manicured fingers on the railing of the bed. Gina was becoming increasingly incoherent by the second.

"Bitch, my son or Hector is not to be touched by you or anyone else." Gina scowled. I laughed, unapologetically.

"Hector touched me in so many places last night and today that he should be registered as a sex offender. Don't worry; I'll take care of him. You should've really taken choice A because B means death." I flaunted.

"Fuck you Bitch!" Gina replied, attempting to get on her feet to mark her territory but the muscle spasms in her back halted her.

"Well suit yourself but remember the way to a man's heart is the same way I'm going to take you out." I walked out of the room as fast as I had come.

Gina angrily grabbed her tray, ignoring Sherry's last threat. Unbeknownst to her, she was contaminating her entire body with every bite. Gina died 20 minutes later.

## Present

"Bitch, did you kill my wife?" Hector growled, gritting his teeth.

"With pleasure and class," I responded with a smile.

Hector roared before jumping up and grabbing a hold of my trachea while he attempted to choke me to death until I produced a razor from the inside of my mouth and began slicing his throat, repeatedly. Hector dropped to the ground, holding his throat as blood seeped through his fingers.

I watched Hector in delight of him taking his last breath before wiping down any trace that I was ever there. I gave him a lipstick printed kiss on the cheek and disappeared into the darkness.

# CHAPTER 12

*"Woooooooh.... Why they had to take him away Lord?*
*Whyyyy????"- Sherry*

## CHIEF MORRIS

3 days later

"Whoever did this shit had to know him personally," I stated in disbelief to my partner, Floyd, as I examined the deep cuts and gashes across the victim's neck and throat area. My eyes traveled from the blood-stained carpet to the feces that wreaked through his clothes, I knew this was not a random murder. "What is his background?" I asked, Floyd.

"Hector Sanchez, 37, widow, single-father, one son. Neighbors expressed they barely saw him out of the house." Floyd replied, recounting back the notes on his pad.

"Run traces of his body any prints around the house. I need anything that can bring forth a suspect." I ordered.

"10-4. I'm on it," Floyd said, jotting down his assignment.

The forensic crew remained very cautious between the broken glass of photographs to refrain from becoming a piece of evidence. The smell that erupted from Hector's body caused everyone to be on the verge of regurgitating.

Floyd took one last look at the scene before he walked out of the house to gather some paperwork. I created two different scenarios in my head that possibly led to this dead corpse.

"This man could've only done one of two things or both, created a bad nemesis or made a scornful woman out of someone to commit a murder, this treacherous." I thought to myself, placing a white sheet over Hector's cold body.

"Anything we can do to help, boss?" Greg and Tony, two rookies from the police academy asked, walking up the stairs and covering their mouths from the overbearing scent.

"Yes, bag him up and locate the kid," I demanded, sucking my teeth at their laziness.

3 hours later

I sat on his desk in deep thought, waiting on the rookies to come back with any source of information but I was becoming extremely impatient.

"How was I going to tell this kid that his father was dead, and he was now an orphan?" I wondered.

"Chief, we found the kid. He is currently a patient at Memorial Hospital in room 445." The rookies announced, out of breath.

"Thanks guys, good work." I dismissively responded.

Greg and Tony looked at each other, noticing the apprehension on my face and walked away.

I was a troubled kid in my youth until my father, Sam Morris, forced me into the police academy or be kicked out of my parent's home. I chose the police academy and have not looked back ever since. I have been in the force for 15 years, graduated to chief and maintained a beautiful family of 3 daughters and a wife who kept me extremely busy.

I made a conscious decision to visit the hospital to deliver the bad news face to face. A phone call would seem too impersonal.

I reached the hospital in record timing to avoid talking myself out of it. To me, this was the hardest part of the job. Each family was different, but they all shared the same hatred for the police like a dog to a mailman. I calmly knocked on the door and a beautiful young lady opened it.

"Yes sir, may I help you? "she asked, confused.

"How are you today, miss? Is this the room of Ramirez Sanchez?" I asked her.

"Yes, is there something I can do to help you?" She inquired, scrunching up her face. The kid in the background spoke up before I had a chance to answer her.

"Loyalty, who's at the door baby?" He asked.

"A cop, who is asking for you." Loyalty responded, scared.

"Well, let him in. I haven't done anything wrong." Ramirez spoke, confidently.

I walked to the foot of the bed where the young man laid and prepared his word usage. Loyalty took her seat right next to him like his protector. Ramirez sat straight up in his bed with a stone face.

"I'm Ramirez, and you are? Have I done something wrong?" Ramirez questioned, uncertain. I could tell that he hated cops by his facial expression and this visit wouldn't make it any better. We the police were the blame, regardless.

"I'm Chief Morris, head of homicide. I'm sorry to be the bearer of bad news, but your father was murdered three days ago. I'm sorry about your loss. We are working around the clock to find a suspect." I stated, sorrowfully.

Ramirez searched my eyes for any untruth but saw none. He went straight into shock mode as he began knocking down the machines that crowded the bed before pulling the IV out and pushing Loyalty off him in an attempt to get to me. Loyalty pushed the emergency button repeatedly and screamed for help. The doctors and nurses busted through the door with a needle to sedate him.

"Hold him down!" Doctor Stephens ordered.

I was not alarmed because this behavior had become something that I was used to after delivering such a mighty blow.

Everyone struggled to grab a hold of him, failing miserably until Dr. Stephens could keep a steady needle in his arm which caused him to calm down, almost instantly. I imagined his legs felt like they were going to sleep. The nurses managed to lay him down as he drifted off into a deep slumber. Loyalty thanked the doctors and nurses for their help as they left.

I gave Loyalty my card and promised to keep in touch with them if I received any further information, regarding this case. I shut the door quietly as Loyalty began praying that Ramirez be granted the serenity, peace, and courage when he lost his last surviving family member that he knew of.

A week and a half later

# Loyalty

The Funeral

"Wooooooooh…. Why they had to take him away Lord? Whyyyy????" Sherry screamed, busting through the doors of Second Arnold Baptist Church in an all-red strapless dress, gold pumps, and a curly wig that paraded her back and a handkerchief. She blew her nose in-between muffled cries. She drunkenly stumbled to the casket, making tons of noise. "Hector, Lord, Hector, the good ones always die so young" were her final words before falling out. Sherry continued.

"If her goal was to win an Oscar, then, she earned that, today, by putting on a performance of a lifetime." I thought.

"Lo, is that your mother?" Quita asked, shaking her head.

"Unfortunately!" I replied, through gritted teeth.

I slouched down in my seat and clutched Ramirez's hand with a tight grip. Everyone looked at each other in unison as if they had never witnessed such chaos.

"You need any help getting up?" The usher asked, reaching out his hands to Sherry.

Sherry swiped his hand away, unapologetically. "No, I don't. Thank you." She got up and brushed off her clothes.

"Uhmmm…" The usher mumbled walking away.

Sherry just rolled her eyes as she spotted a seat next to Shay. "Do you always have to act a damn fool everywhere you go?" Shay asked, cutting her eyes.

"Shut the hell up and move over." Sherry glared.

Bishop Witherspoon decided to preside. "Dearly Beloved, we are here to-day to celebrate, cherish, and share the memories of our brother, Hector Sanchez. I want to give three people the time to honor our loved one. Do we have any volunteers? Also, there is a three-minute limit." He said.

I looked around and saw not one hand raised. "Baby, are you going to say any final words to your father?" I smiled.

I prepared the entire funeral by myself because Ramirez had to be doped up on opiates just to function. Ramirez cried himself to sleep every night following the revelation of his father's passing. The last thing I remembered Ramirez telling him was "I hate you!" which I'm certain held no truth.

"Huh, Bae, I guess I could," Ramirez said, dazed.

Ramirez stood to his feet to a warm audience, clapping their hands as he approached the podium. I hoped he didn't embarrass me as I thought about all the horrific stories Ramirez told me at the hospital about Hector ignoring him, missing his games, and the resentment he accumulated towards him.

"Come on, now, give brother Sanchez a hand." Bishop Witherspoon encouraged, giving Ramirez the microphone. Ramirez looked like he was high in the clouds.

"This is a poem called 'Did you ever love me'. "Ramirez announced.


*Did you ever love me?*
*Every year on Father's Day, I'd wake you up, and asked you to play.*
*You frowned up, scrunched up your face, and pushed me away.*
*Replying very briefly "I'm not your father. No year, No day.*


*What did I ever do to deserve so much pain?*
*I blamed myself every day, eventually driving myself insane*
*especially when you decided not to come to any of my games*
*Have I ever done anything to cause you any shame?*

*No matter what, I still loved you.*
*I just hoped, somewhere in your heart, you loved me too.*
*Ramirez finished with blank stares, and tearful sadness facing him in every direction.*

## SHERRY

I truly felt bad for taking away the boy's father but that only lasted a few minutes until I reflected on the come up that I would receive after Hector's insurance policy cleared in the bank. Once, I took out Ramirez, of course.

After Hector broke my heart and revealed he didn't love me anymore, I vowed to only love one man, and his name was Benjamin Franklin. I came up with the ultimate plan to take out the Sanchez bloodline which was panning out perfectly. I was so caught up in scheming phase two that I missed Bishop Witherspoon's entire message on forgiveness but caught the tail end of it. Maybe if I had, I would be persuaded to forgive everyone that caused me any pain but who am I kidding? I was Sherry fucking Daniels and I didn't give a fuck about anyone but myself, til death do us part.

The Burial

Loyalty, Ramirez, and Quita walked hand in hand to Hector's burial where Bishop Witherspoon recited his final prayer as the drop bury guys were preparing to lower Hector into the ground.

For my final encore, I walked in front of them swiftly to the casket, laying on it before kicking, screaming, and shouting words that were barely audible.

Loyalty shook her head in pure disgust at my drunken behavior but remained still. The shocked expression she possessed during my display of emotion for anyone beside myself, stunned her.

Bishop Witherspoon nodded to both drop bury men to begin lowering the casket even with me on it. They smirked in unison and began to unravel the tight grip knots that kept Hector above ground. I jumped up in horror after realizing I was sinking into the ground as the dirt piled around my feet.

"Help! Help! Help!" I screamed.

The entire congregation erupted in laughter at Sherry's sudden soberness. The crew looked at Bishop for their next task.

"Okay. Get her out." Bishop Witherspoon said lowly, giving dismissal.

Ramirez

"I love you, bae, and thanks for constantly being there for me. You too, Quita" I smiled for the first time in weeks. I loved my new friends who came into my life so unexpectedly and couldn't believe the strength of their loyalty. We all walked away together to the repast, knowing we all had each other which was all that mattered.

Every time something good happened to me, something bad followed. I was so tired of this rollercoaster of life and just can't seem to ever catch a break.

# CHAPTER 13

*Why on God's green earth would your mama name you "Loyalty"
when there isn't shit about you Loyal?"– Ramirez*

## Ramirez

Two weeks later

I returned to school with sympathy cards, gifts, and gestures from the faculty, staff, and students. But to be quite honest, I was tired of hearing that shit. It wasn't going to bring him back. I just hate the fact that I never got a chance to say goodbye! My mind was still wrapped around the fact that I was now, an orphan, and the only family I had was Loyalty.

"I'm sorry to hear about your loss, B." Reggie Holmes, one of my teammates said.

Reggie had called me to the gym earlier to discuss something that couldn't be talked about over the phone for whatever reason.

"What the hell is so urgent?" I thought.

"I appreciate that Reg, but what was so important that it couldn't wait till after school or practice?" I asked, anxiously. Reggie swallowed nervously before deciding to continue.

"What's the deal with you and ole girl, Loyalty?" He asked me.

"That's my shorty. She has changed my life for the better, and I really think she is the one. Why?" I started becoming confused at Reggie's sudden interest with Loyalty. I couldn't help but scratch my head with uncertainty of the correlation between Reggie and Loyalty. Reggie tightened his knuckles.

"He has got to be hiding something." I thought.

"Well, it is a viral video surfacing around school that has Roy, Vincent, and Jordan running a train on Loyalty. I'm sorry, B, but Ole girl, a hoe. I grabbed Reggie by the shirt and jacked him up against the wall before punching him in his throat.  He was scared shitless.

"What the fuck did you just call her? Why do you feel the need to lie to my face? "I gritted my teeth and allowed my anger to get the best of me when I should've gathered all the facts first.

"Come on, B, lie for what?" Reggie handed me his phone from out of his pocket, through my tight grip on his shirt.

I let go of Reggie's shirt and hit play on his phone until I couldn't stomach another second. Angrily, I crushed the phone in my hand and threw it across the gym floor before running to the locker room where Roy, Vincent, and Jordan were passing a joint in rotation.

"What's the deal with yawl running a train on Loyalty? That's some flawed ass, hoe ass shit! Why has nobody ever told me about this bull?" I asked, biting the inside of my gums. They all looked at me like I had five heads and laughed deliriously.

"Yo, B, chill with that name calling shit before shits get real round here. It's not like we owe you any explanation about who we fuck, but, since I fuck with you, I'll kick it to you. Loyalty's mom posted an ad on Facebook, Instagram, and Twitter called "A Night to Remember" and she insisted she had a woman that would do whatever we wanted for the right price. So, shit, we put our money together, gave it to the cougar, and handled our business," Roy, the leader of the crew explained with a smile.

"You got to be shitting me. Show me!" I responded in disbelief.

"I'm as serious as a contestant on 'Fear Factor'," Roy said. Roy scrolled on his Facebook for a few seconds before he stopped and zoomed in and showed me the ad.

It was a silhouette of Loyalty's body from behind in a stripper pose, reminiscent of The Player's Club DVD cover. I saw her body enough times to know that was indeed her but the pain in my heart never subsided. I truly couldn't believe my eyes. Loyalty was the apple of my eye and I wondered to myself, what would make her want to be an escort out of all the things her gorgeous ass could be.

I sped out of the locker room with Roy's phone and ran right into Loyalty while she laughed and talked to Quita in the hallway. How could she be so happy when my heart was ripped in pieces?

"A, Loyalty, you care to explain this shit about you running trains with my teammates. Why on God's green earth would your mama name you "Loyalty" when there isn't shit about you Loyal?" I angrily stated.

Loyalty eyes grew wide and long but this shit was hurting the hell out of me on the inside and showing through my anger on the outside, but I just couldn't fake rock like everything was all good. I could see the huge lump in her throat that refrained her from speaking right away.

"Yo, don't fucking talk to her like that!" Quita demanded, dropping her things to the floor as if she was ready for war. I honestly admired the young warrior because Quita protected Loyalty like a mother protects her cubs.

"What are you talking about?" Loyalty questioned, attempting to defuse the battle between Quita and I. She appeared clueless with tears falling from the inside of her glasses.

I pulled out Roy's phone and played the video from the beginning and couldn't even stomach watching it again so, I let her hold it. Loyalty's face turned red as a hot chili pepper as she covered her mouth in shock. Quita shook her head repeatedly.

"Damn, I never wanted you to find out like this. It's not what you think." Loyalty said, trying to plead her case.

"I……….." she stuttered.

"Oh, shut the fuck up hoe. I can't believe I trusted your grimy ass. You probably stole money out of my father's insurance policy too. I'm glad I never slept with you because I would've had an STD." I said, stopping her in the middle of a sentence.

"If you would let me explain…I can clear all this up!" Loyalty tried to speak AGAIN.

"Bitch get your hoe ass out of my face. You a hoe, a mother-fucking hoe!" I shouted in disbelief, unintentionally creating an audience.

"Hoe! Hoe! Hoe! "The basketball crew chanted repeatedly.

Loyalty ran outside of the school as if she was running for the Olympics. I wanted to run after her because I loved her, but the way my pride was set up, that was Neg-a-tive.

"You could've handled that a whole lot differently. I thought you was a real nigga, but oops, I was wrong." Quita said, before cocking back and punching me dead in my eyes. I fell off impact, seeing stars and red.

"Ooooooooooooooooooooooh." Everyone screamed.

# Quita

I left the scene to look for my friend. I felt that it was a time and place for everything and that was the wrong time and place to humiliate anyone. I know she messed up, but that Hispanic nigga had me fucked up if he thought he was going to carry her like that and Ms. Quita Smalls wasn't going to do anything about it. I wasn't having that, and he knew it.

My knuckles were bleeding and hurting like shit, but I will put them in ice later after checking on my sis. I didn't feel bad at all and would do it all over again. Loyalty was my little sister and I was my sister's keeper. TF?

I spotted a snot-nosed Loyalty, crouched over, regurgitating what she had for lunch in the field. I pulled her up and rocked her back and forth as she cried repeatedly for an hour until she abruptly stopped. How fast she changed, scared me a little.

"I can't turn back the hands of time and if I could, I still wouldn't because if I didn't attempt to commit suicide on that rooftop then, we never would've met. I have a baby on the way regardless so, fuck that nigga." Loyalty said, wiping the tears away with the back of her hand.

I grabbed her face towards mine and said "I'll be the best baby daddy you never had. You don't need anyone that is not going to let you explain your side of the story or carry you like someone he never loved. You are a beautiful queen that deserves the best and I'm going to help you find someone to give it to you. I meant every word.

We went home and turned up for a real nigga. Baby sis was going to be okay if I had anything to do with it.

# CHAPTER 14



## LOYALTY

As I laid in Ms. Small's guest room bed watching "Stepmom" with Julia Roberts and Sara Sarandon, I had an epiphany after watching a scene where Julia gave her stepdaughter an ultimatum about her love life.

"Are you going to cry or do something about it? "Julia asked her c, a brown-haired beauty.

I zoned out of the movie at that point and asked myself the same thing and chose the latter just like Julia's stepdaughter.

It had been over a week since I heard or said anything to Ramirez. I had so much on my mind that I decided to go to Jewels, the juke joint that Ramirez introduced me to on our first date. I missed him greatly, but I honestly didn't have anything to say. The word "Hoe" was still ringing in my ears from the way he talked to me like I wasn't good enough for him as the scum of the entire universe. Ramirez and I not talking hurt me to the core but there was not one thing I could do about it. I jumped out of bed and handled my hygiene to prepare for some serious alone time.

After my shower, I got dressed in a floral jumper and nude sandals. I placed my hair in a tight dreaded bun before applying some nude lipstick and a hint of eyeliner. Satisfied with my look, I gave myself a kiss in the mirror.

"Hey, Qui, can I borrow your car for a couple of hours?" I asked Quita as I walked out of the bathroom, putting the finishing touches to my face.

"Sure. Where are you going?" She asked me.

"Somewhere to clear my head for a bit. Call me, if you need me or your car." I replied and walked out the door.

"Okay be safe," Quita said, sadly.

Quita was really concerned about the demise of Ramirez and I, but she hoped that we worked it out because everyone had skeletons in their closet.

I arrived at Jewels around 8:30 p.m. and the parking lot was jam-packed for poetry night. I brushed the dust from the blunt off my clothes after getting out of the car. I paid my entry/participant fee at the door to the black chiseled bouncer before finding a seat at the bar. Nervousness slowly crept into my bones, but I shook it off quickly.

"Would you like anything to drink?" The bartender asked me.

"No, thanks," I responded and turned towards the stage.

I anxiously waited for the MC to announce my number, so, that I could touch the mic tonight with so much crowding my mind.

"Number 21." The MC finally called out my number.

I grabbed the mic, just as Ramirez drunkenly walked in with bags under his eyes. I was glad he came because this was for him anyway. Him being here made my poem much more personal than just releasing steam.

*"This one is for you. Listen!" I said to him, matching his glare at me.*

*I guess your love fell short?*

*I was a young naïve girl*
*looking for a place in my mother's heart*
*She made me sell my body to the world,*
*but for her love, it was a start.*

*When I grew up*
*I wanted to be just like her*
*I wanted her role*
*I wanted her part*

*I guess your love fell short*
*when you found out*
*I was a wretch*
*I tried to explain it to you*
*but I guess that was too much of  a stretch.*

*My heart was for sale*
*But, as you can see*
*it was never bought*
*I was looking for something in her*
*That she was never taught.*

*You came into my life*
*and made your love unconditional*
*The minute you found out about my past*
*You said your love was purely unintentional*

*If that's the case, I don't want that kind of love,*
*As a matter of fact*
*It should be banned unconstitutional*
*In three months' time,*
*I'll make the love I have for myself,*
*my ritual.*

*To be clear,*
*This is no apology, but a very sincere letter.*
*If you knew the background of my story,*
*Then, you would have loved me better.*

*You've healed my soul*
*And use to caress my pain*
*So, if you never come back,*
*I'll always remember your name.*

Refreshingly, I climbed downstairs feeling like, Kelly Rowland, after exposing my dirty laundry on the stage. I walked swiftly back to my seat before I was stopped, abruptly. He grabbed me by the shoulders with glistening eyes.

"Loyalty, can I talk to you for a second? "He asked me.

My lips curled, and my body tensed in anger. I couldn't believe the audacity he had to touch me.

"Last week, I was "The Help". This week, I'm Loyalty. I couldn't keep up with Ramirez's shenanigans. Especially, not today." I thought.

"Why? So, you can send me on another one of your guilt trips because if so, I already feel bad and don't need any more of your lashings." I said, fed up.

The announcer interrupted his response.

"Will there be any more participants?" The MC asked.

"Yes," Ramirez answered, running to the stage after whispering in the DJ's ears.

"This is for the only woman for me," Ramirez said, blowing me a kiss.

I screamed out loud because Ramirez began singing my favorite song in the entire universe, Chrisette Michele's new slow joint from the "Better" album.

*You mean that much to me*
*Tell me your secrets*
*And I'll tell you mine*
*Every truth, Every lie*
*Every wrong, Every right*
*Every heartbreak, Every setback*
*Every mistake, Every crime*
*Make me your confidant*
*Make me your best friend*
*If you lose or If you win*
*If you're a saint or If you sin*
*And If I don't understand*
*I'll do the best that I can*
*Oh, some people search high and low*
*for someone to make them whole*
*So, I'm not letting go because you mean that much to me. – C. Mi-*
*chelle*

I shed tears of joy knowing that someone loves me just as much as I love him. Ramirez finished with a standing ovation. The song evoked so many emotions from my heart that I knew to be true. Ramirez grabbed a hold of my hand and got down on his knees.

"Loyalty, I don't care what you were baby. I just need you to come home to me." Ramirez begged and pleaded.

I went over his offer a few times in my head and snatched my hand back. I wasn't going back that easy. I had a couple of questions first. TF?

"Ramirez, please don't say things you don't mean. I'm a big girl, and if you want to leave, go ahead and go." I replied, turning my back on him.

"Where can I go, when home is where the heart is?" He responded, melting the ice cubes around my heart.

"Okay, but are you sure you're ready for the whole truth?" I asked, still playing hard to get.

"Yes, Baby, we can talk about whatever you want to. I'm serious as a heart attack." He pleaded.

I turned back around to face him and grabbed his gorgeous face with my bloody-red manicured hands before I said" If you carry me like you did in that hallway, I will slit your pretty throat with my bare hands. Don't fuck with me! Alright?

"Okay… I got it. "Ramirez stuttered.

I got scared myself because I haven't felt like Cookie since I escorted for Sherry. I was so glad Cookie was back. She made me feel so comfortable on the inside.

We both sat atop of Jewel's rooftop to talk. Ramirez was behind me, rubbing my shoulders as I raised my knees under my chin, contemplating how to say what I had to say. This was one conversation that I dreaded, but it was time for me to be a Grown Ass Woman and face the music. I inhaled and exhaled deeply before I began.

"Okay, about six months ago, my mother would dress me up as a grown woman to have sex with anyone, which included students, grandparents, or anybody she could get her hands on because she could no longer make any money off her own body. When you saw me at the party with Quita, I was supposed to be at home servicing some clients. That's why my mother was there in the first place. She has never allowed me to call her mother because she said, "a mother was someone who loved their child and she, on the other hand only loved the money I made for her. Unfortunately, because of my body count, I don't know who my baby's father is, but I know my daughter will not lack any love. Even, if I must do it all alone. I'm sorry that I lacked the courage to tell you the truth but what was I to say, "Hey, I'm Loyalty and I'm a former hoe." My mother was all that I had, and I guess in some weird way I was trying to buy her heart. If you don't want to continue to be with me, I totally understand." I said, all in one breath.

"Stop!!!!" Ramirez placed his hand over my mouth to stop me from continuing." A thousand deaths couldn't keep me away from you. I'm going to help you every step of the way. We are a family."

I smiled, breathed, and sighed as I laid back on his chest to watch the stars.

"Don't worry, my love is free. You and she will be totally fine on my watch." Ramirez added.

# CHAPTER 15

*If I had to kill pretty boy to collect my coins, then his ass*
*gotta go. – Sherry*

## SHERRY

I strutted straight into Richard T. Johnson's office, the executor of Hector's estate with the little ass I had left in a cheap ass black dress that had seen better days that I got from the thrift store. But, hey, at least my hair was done or better yet, I had a wig that covered my missing follicles. I was a woman on a mission and my only concern was collecting these coins, anyway. Nobody, I mean, nobody was going to stand in the way of that. So, if pretty boy Ramirez was trying to stand in the way of my money, then his ass had to go. One way or the other. TF?

I was so elated that phase one of my master plan was over and done with. Killing Hector was so bittersweet for me. Yes, I loved him, but you would be surprised what people will do for the price of money. Hell, he chose a hoe over me and I choose money over his corny ass. The good side of my soul died a long time ago and unfortunately, she was never coming back. I had no pity for the weak because only the strong survived.

"I'm here to see Mr. Johnson for a reading of the will," I said to the young white receptionist. She couldn't have been any more than twenty-one with the Similac I still smelled on her breath.

She rolled her eyes at me like my presence bothered her or something, but I guarantee you she didn't want a piece of Sherry Ashley Daniels. If she didn't put any pep in her step and get Mr. Johnson on the phone jack, I was snatching her ass out of her seat and making her an example for all included.

The receptionist looked at me in disgust as she asked me, "Do you have an appointment?"

"No, I do not, but I know he's expecting me." The receptionist turned around, got on the phone, and began to whisper into the receiver.

My ears perked up when I heard her say something about some gold digging dirty bitch is here to see you. Oh, hell no! It was now on and popping. I jumped behind the desk, crouched over her and jacked her ass up.

"Look, you little uppity bitch. I haven't had my meds in a couple days. So, your best bet is not to fuck with me today before I snap your skinny white ass like a twig from a tree. Are we understood?" I said, through my gritted yellow teeth.

She nodded like a bobblehead to make sure I saw her.

"He... wil…… se...e yo..u no….w." She stuttered, pointing to the door with his name on it.

"Thanks, bitch," I said, while she slowly tried to fix her clothes back up. "Tuh!" I added.

I had no idea why hoes wanted to try me like I wasn't "That Bitch." I rolled my eyes and walked from around the office to the direction of his office. I burst through the door because I was over the invitations. There was no need for me to wait any longer. I was all tried out. Next one that tried me was getting one to the dome. Play with it!

"How may I help you?" Mr. Johnson jumped, pushing his glasses on his face.

"I'm Sherry Ashley Daniels, and I'm here for the reading of the will of Hector Sanchez," I told him proudly.

"Oh, Ms. Daniels, I have been expecting your arrival. I'm elated to see you today. We are just waiting on Mr. Sanchez to appear and then, we will begin. Have a seat." He said to me.

Mr. Johnson appeared shaken by my presence. He stood to his feet in a Gucci imported Italian suit with not a wrinkle in sight. I laughed because as clean as he was, he still had glue on the back of his head from the toupee attached to his skull.

"That's some receptionist." I thought.

He walked to the roundtable and sat in front of me and smiled. I smiled right back at him because business was business.

Ramirez walked in like a supreme Casanova in a black tuxedo, Stacy Adams shoes, and a fresh Caesar haircut to complete his ensemble before sitting next to Mr. Johnson. Sherry shifted herself uneasily in the chair from the nervousness that plagued her.

"Good morning, everyone. Now, let's begin." Mr. Johnson said as he walked to the roundtable and sat in front of Ramirez and me.

I was glad to finally get down to business. I looked at Ramirez with pity because he didn't even know his days were numbered. I knew he wouldn't give me the money without a fight. Loyalty would be heartbroken yet again.

"The last will and testament for Mr. Hector Sanchez are as follows…"

I, <u>Hector Sanchez,</u> of 134 Laurel Green Ct., Savannah, Georgia revoke all former wills and testamentary dispositions made by me and declare this to be my last will and testament.

I appoint, <u>Ramirez Sanchez</u>, to be the sole executor of this will and I give to, <u>Ramirez Sanchez</u> absolutely all my real and personal property whatsoever and wheresoever.

Provided that if <u>Ramirez Sanchez</u>, predeceases me at my death then, I appoint, <u>Sherry Ashley Daniels</u> to be the executor of this will and I give absolutely all my real and personal property to anyone who survived her and alive at my death and if more than one in equal shares absolutely.

In witness of which I have set my hand to this my will this 13th day of October 2017.

Signature by the above-named <u>Hector Sanchez</u> in our presence and by us in his.

*Signature: <u>Hector Sanchez</u>*
*Print Name: <u>Hector Sanchez</u>*
*<u>First Witness</u>*
*Signature: <u>Richard Johnson</u>*
*Print: <u>Richard Johnson</u>*

*<u>Second Witness</u>*
*Signature: <u>Sherry Daniels</u>*
*Print: <u>Sherry Daniels</u>*

I paced the floor repeatedly until phase two was executed in my mind perfectly. I had the perfect plan to exterminate Ramirez that not even Loyalty will be ready when it hits her. Even though I acted like "Billy- Bad Ass", Hector putting me in his will after all I've done to him hit a place in my heart that made me the lowest I have ever felt.! On the inside, I was flattered that Hector would still do that for me after all these years without even knowing if I was alive or married.

A tear escaped out of my eye that I didn't even think I was capable of creating because of Beatrice's last words. I reminisced sadly about the only man that ever loved me back. I wiped my face immediately and transformed back into the bitch yawl love to hate. Hopefully, one day I will be able to tell my version of events. (Wink)

I sat down and wrote down the perfect plan of revenge and left it on my nightstand. I had no room for error. I fell asleep with a deadly smile plastered across my face.

The next day

I browsed through the grocery store looking for something to cook for my "special dinner". I spent about thirty minutes of trying to decipher between two meals in my head before deciding on some Spaghetti, corn, Caesar salad, and Garlic Toast. Tired was an understatement which is why I found the shortest line I could find. Placing my items on the surveyor belt, I almost dropped the Ragu sauce when I realized who the cashier was.

"I just can't believe my luck." I thought.

"Welcome to Harvey's. I'm Ramirez and…." Ramirez stopped mid-sentence when he recognized my face.

" What are you doing here?" He asked, squinting his black bushy eyebrows.

"I got to put on for my city if I'm going to wrap him in my spider web." I thought.

I changed my vibrato into the fakest "white" girl voice I could muster. "I am Loyalty's mother and 2nd in line to your father's estate."

Ramirez gritted his teeth. "You have some nerve showing your face around here when you have a pregnant daughter that needs you."

"Ramirez, is it? I believe we got off on the wrong foot. I would like to invite both of you to dinner on Sunday." I reached out my hand for a handshake, ignoring the part about Loyalty. It seemed like a whole minute before Ramirez shook it.

"What time, Sunday?" He asked inquisitively.

"4:30 will be perfect. We will be having Spaghetti, Texas toast, and Caesar salad. I can't wait to clear the air and reconcile with my flesh and blood over supper because I do miss her. "I faintly smiled for exaggeration purposes.

"Okay, Ms. Daniels, we will be there but don't mess this up because I would hate for you to come up missing due to an unforeseen kidnapping." He smirked.

"That won't be necessary my dear. It's time that I make this right or I will never forgive myself." I admitted.

I walked away ecstatic about my Oscar performance of a lifetime that I couldn't even wait to perform my encore on Sunday.

"Heaven wouldn't have to wait too much longer for another angel. Isn't that what Beyoncé' said?" I thought.

## Loyalty

I sat in Ms. Smalls' guest room with a lot on my mind. Ashanti's "Rain on me" ringtone came on my phone to signal an incoming call. I didn't recognize the number but answered it anyway.

"Hello?" I asked.

"Hey Loyalty, this is Sherry," Sherry responded.

I was two seconds from hanging up because whenever Sherry was around, nothing good ever came about.

"What do you want?" I gritted my teeth.

"Baby, I'm sorry for everything I've done and I'm really trying to make it right." She rushed out of her mouth.

"Oh really, Why now?" I asked, sarcastically.

"Because I'm getting older, wiser, and don't want to die without fixing the damage I've caused, which is why I'm inviting you to dinner at 6, at my house this weekend on Sunday."

I silently reflected on everything Sherry ever did wrong to me. Deep down inside, I still missed her and truly wondered, did she change? I knew there was only way to find out.

"Okay, Sherry, you got one shot, make it count," I responded and hung up.

# CHAPTER 16



*Something you should know, there's something in
my heart. – Michel'le*

## Loyalty

Sleep definitely didn't come easy after that awkward phone call from Sherry yesterday.  Something just didn't sit well with me and in the words of Michel'le "There something I should know because there was something definitely in my heart." In my sixteen years of life, I have never witnessed Sherry to be nice to anyone but Shay. As I laid on my bed waiting on my alarm to hit 8 a.m., my mind raced a thousand miles per minute and I couldn't wait to play "Inspector Gadget" to confirm my suspicions or calm my worries. Either way, I couldn't lay here without figuring something out.

At 8:00 a.m. on the dot, I jumped out of my bed, fully dressed in a red BeBe jumpsuit that Quita bought for me. I walked into the bathroom to put my dreads in a bun and take care of my dental hygiene. Satisfied with my appearance, I left the bathroom to retrieve my "ride or die" so she could ride with me, in case, some shit went down.

"Qui, Qui. Get Up! I have a 911!" I said, nudging her shoulders.

Quita rolled out of bed in a matter of seconds, took the bonnet off her head, and charged to the bathroom. In 4 minutes and 53 seconds flat, she reappeared as if she just had not been sleeping. I swear this was my bitch to the end.

"Wassup, Bitch? What's the tea? Do I need my shank?" Quita rambled.

"I swear I love this girl to death. She is always "TTG" (trained to go)" I thought.

"Slow down, pit-bull! It isn't anything going on yet. Sherry invited me to dinner tomorrow, but something is not sitting well with me about that. Today is Saturday, which means Sherry went to play Bingo with Shay. I hope she still sticks to her redundant schedule. I need an ideal alibi for me to break into her house and find out why I get this uneasy feeling about tomorrow. "I said.

Quita stood in front of me with arms folded and mouth twisted until I finished speaking.

"Say less. Bitch! Let's Ride." Quita responded.

We pulled up fifteen minutes later. My smile widened after noticing Sherry's car was gone. My day was already starting off better than expected. We got out together. It was time to find out what was really good? I grabbed the key from under the brown flat "Welcome" mat and let myself in. After making sure the coast was clear, I grabbed my gloves and handed two to Quita.

"Take downstairs and I will take the upstairs," I told her.

"Got it!" Quita said.

I searched high and low for anything out of the ordinary and came up short. My room still looked the same as I left it, some months back. I grabbed my poetry book from my computer desk and slipped it into my black suede Aldo book-sack. I was starting to think maybe I was just having "cold feet" but I still had Sherry's room to look through before I counted my jitters as part of my imagination.

"Quita, you got anything, sis?" I screamed from upstairs.

"Negative, Captain!" She screamed back.

I inhaled very deeply before turning Sherry's knob. Her room was clean as if she had hired a maid service of some sort. As a matter of fact, the room was the cleanest I had ever seen it. I started checking draws, dresser chest, and everything else. Ten minutes later, I sat down on the edge of the bed defeated. My mind was puzzled and I was so out of breath due to the little one growing inside of me.

I got back up too prematurely to find my balance and ended up knocking over the plastic lamp that sat on the nightstand near me. I picked it up quickly to make sure it wasn't broken or out of place. Satisfied, I placed it back and noticed a small black book with no writing on the cover.  I sat back down and began reading it until I found exactly what I was looking for. I got so caught up into reading that I didn't even notice Quita staring at me.

"I'm guessing you didn't hear anything I said for the past five minutes. "Quita suggested.

I jumped out of my skin, the minute her voice registered in my head.

"Aww, Shit, don't do that to me girl. I thought you were Sherry and I sure didn't hear you but take a look at this. "I answered, handing her the note-book.

While Quita was reading, I jumped up to relieve my frequent bladder that my daughter had given me at "Six- Months." As I began pulling down my underwear, something caught my eye that almost made me urinate on my-self. It was a picture of Ramirez and me kissing at his championship game.

The problem was Ramirez entire head was missing and a caption that read "coming soon!"

"Quitttttttttttttttttttttttttttttaaaaaaaaaaaaaaaaa" I yelled.

Quita busted in through the bathroom door, seconds later with a spooked facial expression. At lost for words, I just pointed. When her eyes traveled in the direction of my finger, she took a step back.

"This is the craziest shit my eyes have ever laid on, especially that book. I guess your suspicions were right after all. What do you plan to do next? "Quita asked.

"Oh, I'm still coming to this "dinner." I have a plan for this bitch. Don't believe me, just watch." I replied.

In a blink of an eye, we put everything back like we found it and vanished.

"I had something coming for her that not even her evil ass would expect." I thought.

# CHAPTER 17



*Go to Hell! Bitch! – Loyalty*

## SHERRY

The sound of the doorbell snapped me out of my thoughts. Instantly, I stopped stirring the spaghetti before running to the bathroom to do a once-over and fix my good wig. I looked at the clock that only read 5:15 p.m. and thought it was a little too early for my company. After fixing my make-up, I pranced to the door seductively in a new black Gucci short dress and matching heels that I bought from the Good-will thrift shop. I looked through the peephole as the doorbell rang again, only irritating the shit out of me. I only saw Ramirez and wondered "Where was Loyalty?" His eyes caused my eyes to flutter as my panties did too!

"I can't make this shit up if I tried." I thought.

I opened the door and smiled.

"Hey Ramirez, where's Loyalty?" I asked, quizzically.

"She's at Quita's house, getting ready and should be here momentarily." He answered, nonchalantly.

"Oh okay. Well, come on in, dinner will be ready soon." I said.

Ramirez walked in, looking all around until his eyes set on the dinner table that consisted of candles and champagne glasses.

"Ms. Sherry, where is your bathroom?" He asked me.

"The third door on the left," I answered, walking towards the kitchen.

Ramirez walked hesitantly into the hallway that led to the restroom. A couple of minutes later, he walked back to the foyer wiping his hands with a paper towel.

"Son-in-law have a drink with me," I stated, extending a glass from the tray in my hand for his reach. Ramirez grabbed the glass and examined it for foul play. I raised my glass in the air for my toast for Ramirez to follow my lead. Ramirez followed suit.

"This toast is for family." I smiled.

After the last gulp from both of us, I grabbed his glass and returned to the kitchen to prepare another round and to turn the food on low.

"So, Ramirez, do you miss your dad?" I asked him.

"Yes, I do." He responded, sadly.

Once, I noticed his changed deposition, I knew that it was time for part two of my plan.

"What is that I see?" I asked him, grabbing his hard-on. He looked back at me with his eyes expanded. "You must be really ready to see me." I continued to taunt. Ramirez's eyes fluttered as if he had no control of his body.

"What did you do to me?" Ramirez groggily mumbled.

"Who, me? I just gave you something to make you feel good."

"You will never get away with this." He said to me.

"I already have." I shot back as I jumped on top of him and slipped my tongue in his mouth. I took off all his clothes and then took off my own.

"Why are you doing this to me?" Ramirez weakly managed to say.

"Because I need that money from the policy, and the only way to do that is to take you out which would make me the next beneficiary," I said.

"You killed him, didn't you?" He asked me.

I smirked deviously. "It was like taking candy from a baby," I smirked.

Ramirez jumped up, pushing me off him to attack but fell due to the effect of the drugs.

"I like it rough daddy." I mounted myself back on top of Ramirez's Mandingo to fill my insides up. "Damn you feel good." I exhaled while riding him in a slow rhythm. Ramirez tried his hardest not to let a moan escape his lips but failed miserably.

"Humph. Damn." He lowly moaned to my extreme wetness, trying not to enjoy it.

"You're even better than your father," I admitted, catching my breath. Ramirez instantly went limp after my last statement. I frowned before beginning to suck on his neck, bringing his erection back into full swing. Ramirez busted the biggest nut of his life inside of me.

"What the fuck is going on, in here?" Loyalty screamed, startling the both of us at once.

# Loyalty

"Baby, I can explain. She drugged me." Ramirez pleaded, but they fell on deaf ears.

All I saw at that moment was red as I lunged towards Sherry, waking up the baby inside of my womb who decided to kick every five minutes, which slowed me down.

"Why, mama? I knew you were up to something. When have you ever made me dinner? I asked, rhetorically. I knocked Sherry to the ground and began stumping the shit out of her with my wheat Timberland boots until she appeared unconscious. Satisfied, I turned on my heels towards Ramirez.

"You did all this to hurt me? Huh? All I ever did was love you, but I guess it wasn't good enough. If she drugged you as you say, why did it look like you were enjoying it? And why is their semen on your stomach?

"Baby, she was trying to kill me to take over my father's estate which will make her super rich. I had nothing to do with this. I swear! "Ramirez cried.

I searched his eyes for the truth and clearly, he was being honest, but I still couldn't get over the semen that lay on top of his stomach. I wobbled to my room, grabbed some tape, and a jump rope. I returned to the dining room and placed Sherry on a dining room chair in the middle of the floor. Sherry started sweating profusely and pleading but this time, I have had enough! I placed the tape on her mouth to stop her from speaking.

"I love you, Loyalty!" Sherry mumbled.

"Aww, Shut the fuck up! You don't love me. You've always loved what I could do for you. There is a major difference. Love is not making your daughter sell her body for your love. Love is not having sex with your daughter's boyfriend. I've got to kill you because if I don't, you will always find a way to hurt me and it's time for you to turn my heart loose." I said, with finality.

"Well, before I leave this world. I got something to tell you… Remember these words… Because I have never loved you a day in your life, you will always suffer from a broken heart." Sherry laughed hysterically.

"You got 60 seconds to get dressed or you're next!" I said to Ramirez. He dragged himself to his feet and began putting on his clothes.

I have never felt so defeated in my entire life. My heart just wouldn't accept another loss. In my heart, I knew what it was time to do. I reflected on every single thing Sherry ever put me through and each situation made me even angrier than the last.

"Can you do me one more favor, Loyalty?" Sherry asked.

"And, what would that be?" I asked.

"Go to hell, Bitch" Sherry boldly stated.

"Right, after you, Bitch!" I shot back.

I walked to the kitchen, grabbed the gasoline and spread it around the whole house, including dousing it on Sherry.

"In a perfect world, we would have the perfect mother and daughter relationship, but your evil spirit deteriorated that for us," I said to Sherry. Sherry didn't shed one tear and just looked at me like she was bored or something. I smirked because I was too ready for the grand finale.

"Let's go Home," I told him. Ramirez looked at me spooked.

"Wait, are you just going to leave her there? "He asked me.

"Let's go, Home. Now!" I said, sternly.

"Okay. Okay. You don't have to tell me twice." He said, with his hands up.

Ramirez opened the front door for me as he bumped into Quita before getting in the car himself.

"Are you done, Quita?" I asked, smiling.

"Yes," Quita answered.

"Great. Ramirez, carry me to the car." I told him.

Ramirez carried me like a ragdoll to the passenger seat in Quita's car.

"Do it now, Quita," I told her.

Quita grabbed a Newport cigarette from the inside of her pocket and lit it before throwing it towards the gasoline as we all watched the house go up in flames. Quita cranked up her engine and pulled off. A tear escaped out of my right eye because I couldn't believe that I would never see my mother alive again. I finally felt liberated that I finally got rid of the one person who just wouldn't turn my poor heart a loose.


The End!

# EPILOGUE

## Loyalty

4 years later

"A moment of clarity appeared in my life, the day you came along, and opened up my eyes, and although I wasn't looking, I came to find, the perfect reflection of, what love should look like," Karina Pasian's "Perfectly Different" lyrics blasted from the speakers as I carefully walked down my fuchsia decorated spiraled staircase at my spacious four-bedroom townhome.

My colors were fuchsia and white. The townhome was decorated in multi-colored crystal rocks and stones. Everybody in attendance was dressed to the tee. I lifted my Donna Karan's fuchsia dress from behind and wrapped it around my hand because it was cut short in the front. I didn't want to be "Michelled" (Destiny's Child) or go on world star with the caption "Bride falls down the stairs in the middle of her wedding."

I was so overcome with emotion that I stopped and looked at my beautiful people around the room from Groves alumni. Even, Ms. Hunter was in attendance. I couldn't believe this many people came out of their way to show their love and support. It had to be over a hundred guests. "Humbled" was an understatement for me. Then it hit me like a ton of bricks, I was getting ready to marry my best friend, lover, partner in crime, Clyde, and most importantly, my husband.

Quita beat my face to death and did my hair in an upwards bun with some braids left out in the front to adorn my face. I don't know where I would be without my girl. She has been there every step of the way. I wanted to just run to her out of fear but what was I so afraid of? She was my go-to for everything and helped me get rid of my ridiculous crooked glasses and replaced them with clear contacts. I winked at her and she threw up the west side hand gesture. I'm convinced she really couldn't help herself.

I wiped my face and straightened up my back when I realized my daughter, Justice Messiah Sanchez was staring back at me with a worried look. Ramirez convinced me to give Justice his last name because she was his daughter too. Even, if not, biologically. He treated her like a fairy princess and like the true Queen she is. I smiled back at her and mouthed "I love her" to put that angelic smile back on her face.

Justice was the spitting image of me. She had a hair that was so hard to maintain because it was so curly. I wanted her to dread up like mommy, but I felt she was too young and had her own brain. Justice inherited my winter-green eyes and lips. Sherry must have really hated me because she looked like her as well. Most days, I didn't think about her and finally mastered the concept of blocking out any history of my past, including memories of her.

Eric Benet's "Spend my life with You" signaling it was finally time to walk down the aisle. Ramirez looked so dapper in his white blazer, fuchsia pants, and shirt. His hair was cut with precision and not a follicle out of place. I smiled because I know I deserved him. He came into my life with his heart on his sleeve and loved me at the lowest point in my life. He changed my life for the better and I couldn't wait to say, "I do". He was a great boyfriend and a wonderful father. Ramirez gave me a sense of purpose in life, love, and his dreams.

We needed each other, unbeknownst to us.

I took my first step off the stairs and sashayed down the aisle in a Tyra Banks-like way. Ramirez started crying and having an episode since he started staring at me. I was relieved because if he didn't I was going to turn around and try it again. The minute my hand touched his, he stopped, and I stood opposite him as the great T.D. Jakes was beginning to preside over us in Holy Matrimony.

Our vows were said to one another in an intimate, elegant, and carefree manner. We had come such a long way together!

"I Now Pronounce the Sanchez's" T.D. Jakes proclaimed as we tongue-kissed each other in the mouth.

I finally found my forever. Now, it was time to take these hard ass shoes off and get ready for the reception.

The reception

We danced our little hearts away. The husband and wife dance with Ramirez had to be my most favorite part. Except for the reality, he had two left feet. Let's just say he was a much better basketball player than he will ever be a dancer.

Justice was asleep in Quita's lap, who was drunk as hell, but jumped up and laid Justice in her chair when she heard her anthem "Gone shake that ass, Ima throw this money." She grabbed the DJ's microphone and became Flavor Flav in a matter of seconds. I couldn't help but laugh and join her. Ramirez joined in too with a microphone of his own. Everybody got on the floor and turned my little house out until the end of the night.

This is the happiest I ever have been in my life. I guess Sherry was wrong because there wasn't any hole or brokenness in my heart. In fact, for the first time in my life, I felt beautiful and wasn't ever going to let no one take that joy from me again.

The next day

Ding, Dong! The doorbell chimed, startling Justice as she played with her dolls.

"Justice, would you get that for mommy?" I asked from the kitchen island. I expected it to be Quita because she frequented my house all the time and Ramirez was at the store and had a key.

I watched as she picked herself from off the ground. "Yes ma'am." She grabbed her favorite doll and headed to the front door. She opened the front door to watch the mailman who left behind a box. Justice grabbed it and shut the door. I met her at the door to retrieve the box.

"Who was that at the door, Justice?" I asked her.

"The mailman." She answered, giving me the package. I went back into the kitchen, unraveling it on the counter. I was kind of skeptical because I hadn't ordered anything. I screamed at the top of my lungs once I had the box opened. Justice ran to the kitchen to where I was standing holding my heart and began to cry when she noticed a burnt hand that contained a note that said

"I'm back."

The Side Effects of a Broken Heart 2: Sherry's Revenge

If you enjoyed The Side Effects of a Broken Heart, Check out an excerpt from my first & second full-fledged Novels:


Poison Ivy: The HIV BANDIT

&

Because you couldn't Love me, I had to Love Myself!

# PROLOGUE

## Ivy

So many thoughts danced in my head. Will the jury finally have enough evidence to convict me this time? I silently wondered to myself. No matter what, I didn't plan to do a second in jail. Not today, not tomorrow, not ever! In fact, I had a pocket pistol attached to the inside of my leg to ensure my escape. I popped my bubblicious Bubblegum and tapped my leg in frustration, but I had no one to blame but myself.

Today, the jury would reach a verdict on me. Allegedly, I was being charged with 10 counts of attempted murder for intentionally transmitting HIV to other people, inflicting bodily harm, aggravated assault, vandalism, trespassing, and a host of other shit. What does that Miranda Law bitch state: I was innocent until proven guilty. That was my story and I was sticking to it. Everything that I did, I had a reason for doing it.

I swiped my bang from my symmetrical bob as a signal to my team to get ready and be prepared for war. My team consisted of what I call the fantastic five: Laila fox as my lawyer, Marvin Gaye as the getaway car who was parked out front, Veronica Mars & Lilia Mae Turner as two Honduran women who posed as civilians on opposite sides in the back of the courtroom, and the devil herself, Me, Ms. Ivy Rae Simmons. I looked at all 12 white members of the jury and by the looks on their faces, I knew that they didn't have one ounce of sympathy for me as they shouldn't because if it's left up to me, none of them will be making it out of this courtroom alive anyway.

I missed my twins, Legacy and Destiny, and I hoped to see them soon. I prayed to Allah quietly in all five of their headsets that we make it out here alive because we had an empire to run. My heart started beating rapidly and my palms were sweating profusely, but I shook it all off as just nervousness. Although this wasn't my first rodeo, I knew it would be my last.

The banging of the gavel silenced my thoughts and prayers simultaneously. I snapped out of the trance I was in to see what this white bitch had to say. Judge Mabeline Wilcox, the crooked out of all crooked.

Judge Wilcox was a middle-aged white woman with red freckles that adorned her face. She put you in the mind of Judge Judy from the red curls on her head down to the glasses and smart remarks. From the way she carried herself, you could tell that she came from old money. She was publicly known for throwing a nigga into jail and throwing away the key. I had her on payroll, but I still couldn't get rid of this gloomy feeling that came over me, so it was time for plan B. I raised three fingers in the air in her direction to remind her that we had her two daughters and husband tied up in a very safe place. In case she tried any funny business. I wired her 50,000 dollars the previous day to an off-shore account in the Netherlands to sway the verdict in my favor. Wilcox immediately turned beet red and gulped very hard after she realized what the notion represented. I had to let her know I was not playing with her ass. She took a huge breath and continued.

"Ms. Fox, did your client hear me?" Wilcox asked Laila as the tears from the brim of her eyes began to surface. I side-eyed Laila, letting her know I heard her, but I was enjoying the cracking of her voice.

"No, your honor. Can you please repeat yourself?" Laila said in my defense. I smirked in a devious manner. The devil in me was awakened as the nice girl from the C-port before me tapped out. The fear in a person's eyes gave me a hard-on I couldn't explain.

"Does your client have any further thing to say until we reach our final ruling?" She sighed, awaiting my response.

I whispered into Laila's diamond-encrusted ears to get this white bitch off my back. Contrary to popular belief, I was not a racist, but people of the law made my ass itch. Laila faced back forward to address this peasant.

"No, she does not. My client assures you and the jury that she is innocent. Do you have any witness present that says otherwise?" Laila countered back.

We all knew the answer to that question was no, as we had already killed all of them. Even if they were, they wouldn't dare show their faces because of the repercussions that would follow.

"No. . She paused. Well, except one that would like to remain anonymous." The judged smirked back.

My heart dropped in the pit of my stomach as I knew exactly who this mystery person was. Fuck it, there was no turning back now. I kept my game face on regardless. I wouldn't dare let this bitch see me sweat.

"Do you have any concrete evidence? Laila asked with uncertainty."

"As a matter of fact, we do, we have surveillance video of your client doing some of the things she has been accused of. Wilcox nodded her head to no one in particular.

The bailiff pulled a television out of the corner of the room and placed it diagonally in front of us and mashed play for all to see. My eyes could not believe they caught me red-handed injecting HIV needles into the victim's arms and killing them all execution style.

I guess her making partner was more important than keeping her family alive. Shame on her. I hoped she kissed them goodbye because that was the kiss of death. I pressed the button on my watch, igniting the bombs across their bodies back at the warehouse, silencing their lives forever.

"We, the jury of New York find Ivy Rae Simmons, Guillllll….

"Now!" I screamed, stopping Wilcox from finishing her sentence.

Veronica and Lilia arose from their seats, snatching the garments from their face, replacing it with their night vision goggles and smoke mask before throwing smoke bombs on both sides of the courtroom as Laila and I ran and back-flipped to the emergency exits that were placed behind us. Lilia shot the judge and bailiff in between their eyes, killing them instantly while Veronica threw a grenade in the jurors' direction, blowing their bodies apart. Satisfied with their work, they vanished, leaving a gruesome scene behind.

Before you judge me, get to know me. Let's go on this journey together. This will be my one and only time explaining myself. Gear up for one of the greatest stories ever told. Love me or hate me because personally, I don't give a fuck. When you get to the last page, see if you feel the same way. I knew you would've done the same damn thing if you were placed in my shoes. Enough rambling.

This is:

Poison Ivy: The HIV Bandit.

I don't why when he hurts me, I'm still here,
And why do I love him through these tears?
Maybe cause' we been together all these years
And me being alone is my one true fear.
– Ashanti

# PROLOGUE

## SOLO

The Sunlight kissed my white fluorescent veil that was carefully placed on my head to prevent my black spiraled curls from falling everywhere due to the heavy winds of the Turks island we were on for holy matrimony. I stood up straight and narrow in my custom-made Vera Wang white flowered symmetrical dress which turned out to be difficult because of the electricity that shot through my body causing me to feel wedding jitters that I hope my stepfather Willie didn't notice as we slowly walked down the aisle of marble prepared for us.

"Are you okay baby girl?" Willie asked with a concerned facial expression.

"Yes. Daddy, Thank you." I responded with a sly grin to put his mind at ease.

The tears instantly started coming as I looked ahead at the man of my dreams: Mr. Terrance James (Sr.). I couldn't believe that he finally popped the question after all these years.

Terrance was dressed in navy-blue trousers, a baby blue shirt with some brown Birkenstocks. He owned a box cut that was tapered to perfection. Honestly, I had never met a man that possessed such natural beauty. I couldn't help but feel embarrassed as I watched Teddy, his best man, and best friend grab his shoulders to get his attention while he held his head down playing with his feet. I thought that was rather odd because our wedding song, "If Only You Knew" by Patti Labelle had already begun and everyone was already on their toes. We had been practicing for the past week so I had no idea what the hell was going on but I was about to find out. Maybe something was just on his mind. I was hoping like hell he didn't embarrass me at this altar. As Terrance lifted his head, he had a lost impression etched on his beautiful face.

My gut told me something was wrong but again I shook it off. Willie let my hand go, gave me a peck on the cheek, and returned to the groom's side of the wedding party. We had my wonderful biological father, Bishop Mohammad Brown presiding over our island-themed ceremony. I winked at my bridesmaids and maid of honor Tammy before grabbing Terrance's hand to calm his anxiety so that he could focus on me.

My father was now ready to start the ceremony "We are gathered here today to join the forces of holy matrimony of Solo Denise Brown & Terrance Moses James…" We had gotten all the way down to reciting our vows but it wasn't until the moment Terrance James Junior, my three-year-old son walked down the aisle to bring our rings that I lost it. He was the greatest gift I ever received in this relationship. TJ smiled at us with a toothless grin making the crowd "Aww" in unison.

"If any of you has reasons why these two should not be married, speak now or forever hold your peace." My father asked the audience.

"I do." Someone spoke from the crowd.

"Noooooooooooooooooooooooooooooooooooooooo," I screamed.

I jumped out of my sleep to the sounds of my 7:00 a.m. alarm ringing. That dream occurred in my sleep almost daily. I heard it but could not see it because my eyes were swollen shut. I felt around the bed to see if

Terrance stayed but after feeling his side of the bed, my question was answered. Then, slowly all the events of last night came running back to me.

Last Night

I was in the kitchen preparing mash potatoes with gravy, sweet peas, and pork chops while TJ sat at the table behind me doing his homework. Terrance had not gotten home yet so I wondered where he was at. I grabbed my phone to shoot him a text.

Me: Where are you?

Terrance: On the Way

Me: Well, hurry up, we miss you.

He sent me a read receipt but didn't respond. I decided not to get upset because I planned to have a good night that ended in some long overdue sex.

Fifteen minutes later, Terrance walked in wearing his Nike jumpsuit as if he had been to the gym. He dropped his gym bag off in the foyer and bypassed us without even speaking. I turned the food on low to find out what was his problem and told TJ "I'll be right back."

He replied, "Okay, Mommy."

Like a woman on a mission, I peeked in every room until I found him on the edge of our bed hunched over in deep thought as he didn't even notice me come in. I silently asked the "most high" to give me the strength because I just knew it was going to be a long night.

"Hey. What is your problem? Why didn't you speak to us when you walked in, and what are you in here thinkin' about?" I rambled off.

Terrance looked at me with a blank stare but still said nothing. I was starting to get agitated and began waving my hand in front of his face before I said "Hello, can you hear me? Earth to Terrance."

"Yes, I can hear you? The question is "Do I want to?" The answer to that will be hell No!" He angrily replied.

Inside, I wanted to have a peaceful good night but it just didn't seem like that was going to happen anymore due to his angry outburst. I was so consumed with the next thing I was about to say that I didn't even notice the silent tears that streamed from his beautiful face.

"What's wrong baby?" I asked.

He placed his hands over his face like he had the weight of the world on his shoulders. Then, his phone started ringing. Terrance picked it up to see who it was and placed it back down. I picked up the phone to see if I could identify the number because it wasn't saved but couldn't recall ever seeing it so I gave up and put the phone on the dresser.

I went to check on TJ for ten minutes and came right back. When I entered the room again, Terrance seemed like he had calmed down and was ready to talk. "Solo, I have a question." He said.

"What is it?" I asked.

"What would you give for pure happiness?" He asked. I thought it over for a second.

"Anything and everything," I answered truthfully.

"Good. Now, I have another one." He said looking me square in my eyes.

I was starting to get nervous because I didn't know where this conversation was headed but I was no punk, so I was ready for whatever.

"Okay, I'm ready." I shot back with my arms folded across my chest.

"Have you ever lived your life in fear of what others may say about you? Friends, family, etc.?" Terrance asked.

"No, I haven't," I answered.

"Well, I have and I don't want to do it anymore. Besides, I'm in love. Unfortunately, it's not with you." He said without an ounce of remorse and the biggest Kool-Aid smile that I had ever seen him muster. He was almost blushing.

I was crushed and speechless to the point that it felt like the wind was knocked out of my chest. This is the only man I had ever been with and here he was telling me this bullshit. I wanted answers and NOW! I replayed every word he just said and knew my ears were playing tricks on me.

"Terrance, who is this woman? How long have you guys been messing around? Is she white, black, or Chinese? How did you meet? Where does she live?" I questioned back to back. Even though, none of the answers would make my heart feel any better or any less useless.

"None of those answers are relevant. The only thing that should matter to you is that I'm owning up to my shit and telling you the truth. F.Y.I, there is no woman." He replied.

"There is no woman." I repeatedly played back to myself until my eyes grew as big as saucers.

"Wait, you're gay?" I asked hypothetically.

"Yes, I am. I have been gay all my life. You and TJ was just a cover-up not to raise any suspicions to my 'holier-than-thou' father. Don't get me wrong. I love you but I'm in love with him. I'm sorry but it is what it is." He boasted like he didn't have a care in this world.

I slid down the wall crying tears of my own, thinking about all the special moments we shared for it all to come down to this moment. I looked around the room for something to make me feel better until my eyes landed on my tall white lamp that stood on the right side of my foot. Minute by minute, I grew angrier and knew I was about to SNAP. I grabbed the lamp from the bottom up, leaped forward and smashed it to the left side of his head. His head flew back from the impact before he could realize what had happened. Terrance raised his head as blood began to leak down his face and a sign of blood on his ears. His eyes bulged at the sight of blood running from the right side of his left hand before he lost it and began jumping on me wildly. He started landing punches anywhere that he could, starting with my eyes. Eventually, I managed to climb in a fetal position until I heard TJ screaming trying to pull Terrance off me.

"Daddy, you are hurting mommy! Please get off her! "He cried. TJ used all the strength his young body had to pull on his father's leg. Terrance snapped out of his trance and got up. TJ fell over in the process.

"Yo, I'm out. I can't believe you put your fucking hands on me." He said in disbelief, grabbing his suitcase that I didn't see until now. I grabbed TJ and placed him over my chest to be sure he wouldn't attack again.

"What about your son? Did you ever consider him in your decision making?" I asked. He turned around, remaining silent and stone-faced as my mind went in severe brain overload.

I was still hoping to change his mind. Even, if it came down to begging him to stay. There wasn't any shame in my game for someone I truly loved or valued in my life. Hell, I needed him. I wasn't strong enough to do this on my own. My entire life revolved around this man but here he was confessing his love for someone else, let alone, a man. Hopefully, there was some type of compromise we could adhere to or was it just wishful thinking?

I watched him put one foot out the door and screamed: "Wait!" Terrance turned back with a scowl that didn't faze the last trick up my sleeve that I had left. "I need you. We need you. Please don't leave us here alone. We can make this work if you try." I pleaded with tears streaming down both of my cheeks and snot running from my nose.

He left out the door and took my heart with him…

Interested in Writing and/or Publishing a book?
Visit us @ www.a2zbookspublishing.net

To my supporters, I thank you for taking the time out to purchase this book. Your support means everything to me and the reason I keep going.

You can contact me by social media and email:

IG: @astoldbyscar

Email: scarlettjolai1994@outlook.com